THE COURT REPORTER
ALWAYS GETS THE LAST WORD

Amy,

Thank you,

Sam

Also by Pamela Dehnke:

Cabin 12: A Sorority Sisters Mystery
Wrong Place, Wrong Time, Prequel to the Court
Reporter Mystery Series

The Diary of An Extraordinarily Ordinary Woman

And Her Rather Eccentric Sister

And coming soon:

Book Two in the Court Reporter Mystery Series
to be released in September, 2024.

THE COURT REPORTER
ALWAYS GETS THE LAST WORD

By Pamela Dehnke

First edition, 2024

First printing, 2024

Cover design Karen Phillips

Cover background Karen Phillips

This is a work of fiction. Names, characters, places, and incidences are either the product of the author's imagination or are used fictitiously, and any resemblance to actual persons, living or dead, business establishments, events, or locales is entirely coincidental.

Library of Congress in Cataloging-in-Publication Data

ISBN: 9798335022026

Dehnke, Pamela

Dedication

To my brother, Dale Willard Dehnke,
May 18, 1948 – May 18, 1971

Author's Note

I enjoyed a career as a court reporter for thirty years, reporting depositions in the San Francisco and Los Angeles areas. I spent days in attorneys' conference rooms taking down testimony on my little machine, while looking out at the Golden Gate Bridge or the Los Angeles skyline. To me, reporting was like playing a word game all day and getting paid for it. I retired because the traffic in the metropolitan cities had me spending too many hours on the freeways.

I wasn't ready to slow down yet, so I purchased Nightingales Bed and Breakfast in Ashland, Oregon, a charming town where my family, friends and I had spent endless summers seeing incredible productions at the Oregon Shakespeare Festival. Welcoming guests at the B&B has been a delight, but I missed reporting, so I decided to write about it in the genre I love most: mysteries.

I hope you enjoy reading about Addie and her thrilling and humorous adventures in the legal world as much as I enjoy writing them.

Table of Contents

Chapter 1: The Court Reporter Always Gets the Last Word

Wednesday, October 2, 1996

"You're a scumbag attorney!" our witness, Mr. Baxter, yelled as he flew across the table, knocking over a bowl of Halloween candy and choking the opposing counsel.

The court reporter always gets the last word, so, with my little court reporting machine in front of me, I typed, "Witness jumps across table and begins choking Counsel Jones, 3:57 p.m. Off the record." The witness's counsel tried pulling his client off Jonesy as I yelled out of the conference room, "Security, stat!"

A burly Black guy named Tommy rushed into the room and yanked the witness off Jonesy. Tommy handcuffed Baxter's hands behind his back, which was no easy feat as Baxter is a large, lumbering sort of man; he reminds me of a bear.

"I'm going to kill you and that asshole you work for. He's a liar and a cheat," Baxter continued yelling.

Tommy addressed the witness's counsel. "Follow me down to the security office so you can chat with your client about how nasty jail cells are."

When the door closed behind them, I said, "Hey, Jonesy, are you all right? You're looking a bit green."

"Nah, I'm good. Took me by surprise, is all. Here I thought being an attorney would be a gentleman's career."

We'd been taking a deposition, which is the process of a witness giving sworn testimony under oath. The depo took place at the Law Offices of Larry L. Larceny, Esq., otherwise known as Lars, who chose that moment to walk into the conference room and ask, "How did the depo go?"

Lars is about five foot ten. He's a slouch. His suits are baggy on his skinny frame, and they look like he slept in them. He always wears a kippah. He wants people to think he's a pious Jew and an honest man. He's got a non-descript face, almost like one of those dolls without facial features, and I've never seen him smile.

Jonesy laughed. "You just missed the excitement. Baxter leapt across the table and started choking me. Fortunately, Addie called for security, and Tommy got the guy off me. He says we're scumbag attorneys. He thinks we're defrauding Medi-Cal and causing his mother to be in a subacute nursing facility longer than necessary."

"He's crazy. I want to settle this case. It's getting out of hand," Lars replied.

Lars's secretary Norma entered the conference room as I gathered the Halloween candy. "This envelope was just delivered. It's addressed to you, Lars." She handed it to him and quickly left the room to answer the ringing reception phone.

Lars opened it and frowned as he read. Slowly, he replaced the note in the envelope and, lost in thought, began slapping it against the palm of his hand. Just then his mobile phone began ringing, and scowling, he dropped the envelope on the table while he fumbled in his many pockets to locate his phone. He answered agitatedly, "Hello! Yes!" and left the room.

Jonesy is young and naive. He's dark and handsome, short of stature, and dresses impeccably. Larceny hired him right out of law school. This is his second case. It's a Medi-Cal fraud suit, and I've reported most of the depos thus far. Basically, a bunch of people are suing Lars for mismanaging their Medi-Cal cases. I don't usually work for him, but Jonesy requested I report his depositions. He'd worked against me on his first case and found that he really liked me, as well as my brother, Dale, who also happens to be an attorney. Sounds odd, I know, but Jonesy represented my sister, Missy, who'd decided to sue my brother and me, as well as our mom and her attorney, over Mom's will and trust.

Mom is alive and well, other than being legally blind due to macular degeneration, which at this point means she can't drive. She can still see well enough to read large print, play bridge, and play "at" tennis. She'd put her income property in Dale's and my names when she realized her limitations would most likely only worsen. Mom didn't want Missy to have the property because she'd sell it, but she asked us to pay Missy her fair share of the market value of the property. Little Missy, however, took offense and refused to accept the money, preferring to sue us in the hopes of getting the property in her name only. It was just another frivolous lawsuit.

Jonesy gathered up his notes and files. The color was returning to his face. I began packing up my equipment.

"Need this transcript expedited, Jonesy?" I asked.

"Yeah, can you get it to me tomorrow? I think I'll file a motion."

"You got it. I love expedites. That's where the big bucks are. Maybe if I save enough money, I can buy a red Maserati like yours. You've got to take me for a spin in that baby one of these days."

"How about now? I've had enough excitement for one day. I'll take you for a ride around the block, and we can still beat the traffic out to the beach." Jonesy lives in Topanga Canyon, California, just off Pacific Coast Highway, overlooking the ocean. I live in Santa Monica, seven blocks from the beach.

"Sounds good. Let me get this equipment in my car, and I'll meet you in the security parking level in fifteen minutes."

Before leaving, I collected the documents marked in evidence. The reporter is responsible for the exhibits, as well as the transcript, and their safe delivery to the court; therefore, I usually don't let anyone leave the room until I'm sure I've got all the exhibits. It occasionally happens that one or two exhibits unwittingly get caught up in an attorney's files. I had all thirty-three, some paper-clipped together and in a bit of a mess, but I decided to sort through them later. Thank goodness I didn't have to go chasing one of the attorneys to retrieve a missing document, which I'd had to do on a few occasions.

I got my DataWriter, the small machine that I take testimony on; my tripod, which the DataWriter sits on right in front of me; my laptop, which I place on the conference room table at arm's length; exhibit stickers; and cables and such packed into my nifty rolling bag and headed for the elevators.

Hanging witches and bats decorated the elevator lobby, and as the elevator door opened, a ghost jumped out at me. The ghost was a sheet propelled back and forth by an air gun. It seemed a bit over the top, but what the heck? I imagine that people working for a law firm need some comic relief.

I put my equipment in the trunk of my car and took another elevator up to the security level. Jonesy was there waiting. I jumped in his car, and we drove around a few blocks, chatting about this and that. Arriving back at the parking garage, I thanked him for the ride.

"I love your car. It will be a while before I can afford one, though. I'm still recovering from Kat's college expenses."

"How does she like teaching at Lewis and Clark?"

"She loves it. You know, I wanted to be a college professor. I was working on my master's degree in English lit when my husband died. Suddenly, I was the sole provider for Kat and myself. My mother's uncle had done quite well financially as a court reporter during the Great Depression, so I enrolled in a court reporting college, thinking that I would work at reporting while I finished my master's and went on to get my Ph.D., but I loved the job so much I never went back. Maybe someday."

"I know what you mean, Addie. I love the law. That's why I'm going to be leaving Larceny."

"That's wonderful news," I said, "and about time. I know you found out what a conniving cheat Lars is when you were working on our case and he had Missy forge Mother's signature on documents. Missy should have gone to jail, but, of course, he knew we wouldn't let that happen. As hateful as Missy can be, we try to protect her. Some people think she has mental health issues, but she doesn't. She's just plain stupid, and as mean as a junkyard dog. Lars's worst trick, though, was demanding production of documents at 4:45 on Friday afternoon."

"He asked me to cross the line once too many times. Lars has gone way over the top doing spiteful things that are just on the edge of the law," Jonesy said.

"How about the time he froze my government-protected Keogh account without a court order?" I added. "I thought my brother would blow a gasket. Lars has a rep for being the biggest fraudster in Los Angeles, but he hasn't been caught with his hand in the cookie jar, not yet anyway. Have you taken a position with another law firm?"

"Yes, I'm going with the Oakley Firm in San Francisco," Jonesy replied.

"Oh, they're fantastic. I did some depos with them a few years back. You'll love working there. It's a good fit for you, and San Francisco is an awesome place to live," I said.

"It sure is," he commented. "I'm a theater nut, like you, so I'll be in my element."

"You certainly will," I agreed. "I'd better have one of the parking attendants bring my car up and let you get on your way. I'll get the transcript to you in the morning. Have a great evening."

As I drove out of the parking lot, I had no idea how drastically my life would change in the next forty-eight hours.

* * *

The traffic in Topanga Canyon going from the Valley to the beach was slower than molasses in January. It wasn't moving any faster in the opposite direction either. I was anxious to get home, get this transcript out to my scopist, Patrice, and have a little downtime. Patrice cleans up my transcripts for me, checking punctuation, spelling, grammatical errors, stuff like that. She loves expedites as much as I do. We have to get the transcript out eventually. We might as well do it right away and get paid double.

As I slowly wove my way around the curvy road, I realized I'd lost sight of Jonesy. The way that Maserati handles, he was probably home by now. Living in the canyon, he's closer to home than I am living in Santa Monica.

Suddenly, a loud explosion rattled and shook the car. My heart pounded. I concentrated on keeping my car steady while people pulled off the road, and smoke rose from the canyon below. I stopped in a pullout and jumped out, joining the people looking over the edge of the canyon.

"A car swerved and hit the barrier, spinning down into the canyon," someone said.

The black smoke was so thick we couldn't see anything.

"No one could have lived through that," someone else yelled out, coughing.

The smoke drove us back away from the edge. Screaming sirens made it impossible to hear what anyone said. The police arrived and asked us to clear the area. I got in my car and joined the line of cars heading toward PCH. I kept thinking about the people in the car. How frightened they must have been, sailing into the air and dropping into the canyon below, knowing their lives would suddenly be extinguished.

Chapter 2: Gabe

Still Wednesday

It was a beautiful October evening in Santa Monica—October being my favorite month. Though our seasons are not very pronounced here on the Southern California Coast, the leaves on the trees were beginning to turn into their vibrant oranges, reds, and yellows, denoting October, Halloween, the onset of fall, and the holiday season ahead.

As my home came into view, I was reminded of my good fortune. I love this place filled with memories of happy times. Its beauty and charm never fail to take my breath away. My parents bought this property, an upper and lower flat on Seventh and Marguerita, in 1954 when Dad flew the first helicopter into California. The house was a gift from them for my fortieth birthday, the same year I passed the State Board exams to practice as a court reporter. I live in the upper flat where we lived when I was a child, and I lease out the lower flat to my assistant extraordinaire, Jaime. He oversees all my scheduling and billing and keeps my life organized. He and his partner, Chris, also help keep my mom out of trouble. She lives in the cottage on the side of the property.

Jaime is fifty-eight, about five-ten, strong and muscular, with ashy blond hair beginning to streak with a little gray. He keeps it short in what they used to call a brush cut. He has jade-green eyes that catch you in their grip. His favorite outfits are jeans and white T-shirts, and he's most often seen wearing moccasins, which he calls his "house shoes."

I first met Jaime's partner, Chris, when I had my hair done for my senior high school pictures. I'd been getting my hair cut at a little shop on Montana Avenue, but for my senior pictures, I wanted to go somewhere more upscale. I got an appointment with Chris at a salon on San Vicente, and I never went back to the little shop on Montana Ave.

I fell in love with Chris. His appearance is almost the complete opposite of Jaime's. Chris is sixty-four, six-foot-two with short, dark, wavy hair. One eye is forest-green and one is deep brown, a highly unusual combination, which often discombobulates people, but it's a terrific conversation starter. He's of medium build and dresses in classic tailored pants, shirts, and sweaters. He wears penny loafers. He's British, and one would think he came from royal lineage.

As I pulled into the garage, I noticed that Jaime and Chris had been busy putting out Halloween decorations. They love decorating and always start early. Everything was lit up. Witches flew around on brooms. Large, smiling pumpkins hopped around the yard. Ghosts peeked out from behind the bushes. Black cats skidded here and there across the lawn. How did they manage to make it all look so real and inviting?

I walked through the door just after seven o'clock, where I was greeted by my two Siamese cats, Law and Order, who bawled me out for arriving home so late. I slipped into my comfy UGG slippers and headed for the kitchen, where I gave the monsters some canned food to keep them at bay. Then I went to my wine cellar, chose a lovely bottle of Jordan Chardonnay and proceeded to pour myself a glass. I'd recently visited Jordan Winery and was quite impressed with their wines. I even joined their wine club and brought back a case.

My office overlooks our beautiful garden and Mom's cottage and makes it easy to keep an eye on her comings and goings. I unpacked my laptop and sent the file of today's proceedings to Patrice. Finally, I walked into the living room and relaxed in my favorite chair next to the fireplace. With a push of a button, I lit the fireplace and picked up my knitting before turning on the television to check the news. They were covering the crash in Topanga Canyon. I couldn't believe my eyes when I saw Jonesy's Maserati—what was left of it. It was almost unrecognizable. The newscaster said they'd recovered only one body, and they were unable to release identity at this time, but I knew it was Jonesy. I felt sick to my stomach.

***

I spent a restless night. Jonesy's accident brought up nightmares about Gabe. Gabe and I had dated for four years and had just gotten engaged when he went missing in an FBI sting operation gone bad. He was presumed dead after last being seen in front of a building that exploded in a fiery rage. My repetitive dream is that Gabe's still alive, but he's badly hurt and unable to find me. Sometimes he's in a wheelchair. Sometimes he suffers from amnesia. I reach for him, touching his fingers, but he slips out of my reach and disappears.

We met at a birding festival, something I occasionally attend with friends who are quite serious birders. I'd only just arrived in Dallas at seven o'clock in the morning, having taken a redeye flight from LAX. By the time I got to the hotel, it was going on nine o'clock. I had the bellhop hold my luggage because I wanted to catch the nine o'clock lecture on Migratory Journeys. I came into the room late, and the only chair available was a beanbag seat in the back of the room, which, in my condition, was a destination for disaster. I promptly fell asleep and was awakened by a man that took my breath away. He was six feet tall, dressed in jeans with a white shirt and an aviator jacket. His sandy-blond hair was cut in a classic short style. When I woke to his gentle touch and his piercing, sky-blue eyes staring into mine, I thought I'd tumbled into a thrilling blue corridor.

"Are you alright?" he asked.

"Ye—yes, I am. I fell asleep. How embarrassing."

"I don't think anyone noticed because most of them were asleep, too. You certainly didn't miss anything."

I was attempting to gracefully get myself up out of the beanbag chair. "I wonder why they have all these beanbag chairs in the back of the room," I commented.

He reached a hand down and pulled me up. His touch was seductive, and I suddenly felt like the room was a bit too warm. "They were used for the previous event in this room, but for the lecture we were here to attend, they're an invitation to nap for those of us who came in late. Can I buy you a cup of coffee?"

"Yes. That sounds terrific. I'm in dire need. My name is Addie Henkey, by the way."

"Gabe Trusdale."

We began walking toward the coffee shop.

"When I was a kid, there was a Trusdale family that lived down the street from us on Marguerita in Santa Monica."

"That was my aunt and uncle and cousins. Aunt Judy and Mother are sisters and very close. We used to spend most of our summers with them. For us kids, the beach was our summer playground," he said, reminiscing.

"Oh, my goodness! Ours, too. I still live in the house on Marguerita, and my brother lives in the old Kniss house on the beach. What a coincidence. I remember the Trusdales moved back to Long Island the year before we went into high school. Are you from Long Island as well?"

"Yes, originally. I've moved around through the years. Now I have a home on Catalina Island."

"I love Catalina. My daughter and I used to spend a few weeks there with some friends every summer. What's it like to live there?"

"I'm up in the hills just above the Zane Grey Pueblo Hotel. It's peaceful, and I have an incredible view of Avalon, the harbor, and the beach. It's my sanctuary."

"It sounds lovely, and what a great place for birding," I commented. "Are you an avid birder?"

"Actually, I'm not. I've always been interested, though, so I thought I'd sit in on some of the lectures while in town, and I'm glad I did."

We sat in a booth, ordered coffee, and continued talking. I asked, "Are you in town on business or pleasure?"

"A little of both," he replied, as his sky-blue eyes bored into mine. "What about you? Just here for the birding festival?"

"Yes," I answered. Those eyes were making my heart beat a bit faster than normal. "I occasionally meet friends at a birding event, thinking I'll become a serious birder, but so far, it hasn't happened."

"Henkey...Henkey. That's such a familiar name. Is your father Will Henkey, the famous aviator?"

"Yes, he is."

"And your brother is Dale Henkey, the kid that received all the medals from his service in Vietnam?"

"That's my baby brother. Although, he's hardly a kid anymore," I said, smiling.

"Didn't you have a whacked-out sister, too?"

I laughed. "Oh, yes. Missy is alive, well, and still whacked out. How do you remember so much about my family? I certainly would have remembered you."

"We all played together down at the Jonathan Club. They used to call me Baby Gaby. Terrible nickname," he said, grimacing.

"You're Baby Gaby?"

"In the flesh."

"Jumpin' jupiters! The kids used to call you that because you wouldn't go in the water. I felt so sorry for you. Did you ever overcome your fear of water?"

"Well, yes, somewhat. I was a Navy SEAL during the Vietnam War."

"Oh my gosh! You sure did get past your water issues."

We continued talking until we noticed the lunch crowd beginning to arrive, whereupon we ordered sandwiches and spent another hour and a half together. Finally, I said, "I think I'd better check in with my friends and get cleaned up. Would you like to join us for dinner?"

"I'd be delighted," Gabe replied. "How about we meet in the bar for a cocktail, say six-ish?"

"Sounds good! I'm a staunch believer in cocktail hour," I said, as my body sent me delightful sensations when Gabe looked into my eyes.

Chapter 3: Ali and Able
Thursday, October 3, 1996

I crawled out of bed, being careful not to disturb Law and Order. While I waited my obligatory three minutes for the coffee press to bring my coffee to perfection, I did a few yoga poses. I took the coffee into my office. Patrice had emailed the completed transcript to me, but now that Jonesey was dead I wasn't sure who should get the transcript and the documents in evidence that were attached. I took it all down to Jaime to assemble and bill out and then decided to call Lars's office assistant to see is I should send the transcript to Lars or if he'd already assigned Jonesey's cases to another attorney in the office.

"Good morning, Norma. How are you doing? I heard about Jonesy's crash on the news last night. Such a tragic accident. I can hardly believe it. I went for a ride with him just before he headed over the canyon. In fact, I was close behind him, but he got ahead of me. Do they know how the accident happened?"

Norma's voice caught. "No. I haven't spoken to anyone. It's too soon. Lars just arrived. You'd think he'd close the office for the day due to Jonesy's death, but he didn't. He has a depo at ten, and the court reporter he usually uses just called to say she has a family emergency and can't make it. Is there any chance you can report this depo? I'm desperate.

Lars is going to be furious because this is an important case. I'll buy lunch."

"Sure. Depending on our infamous LA traffic, I'll be there in about an hour and a half. And I'll bring the transcript of yesterday's deposition with me. Jonesy had asked to have it expedited for this morning because he was going to file a motion."

***

Arriving at Lars's offices in record time, I greeted Norma. "Good morning. I'll just go in the conference room and set up."

"We have to do this depo in Larceny's office," Norma replied. "Someone else is using the conference room today. Follow me."

"Okay," I said.

Norma is a lovely, young Puerto Rican gal, about seven or eight months pregnant.

She often wears her long, black hair in a bun. Even with the extra pregnancy weight, she's curvaceous and sexy, having what the boys used to call bedroom eyes.

As I wheeled my equipment down the hallway, I noticed a lot of vacant offices. Despite Lars's unorthodox legal practices, I thought his business was doing all right, but this didn't bode well. Maybe he's renting out the conference room for the extra cash flow. It's not uncommon with small law firms.

"Right in here," Norma said.

"Holy cow!" I exclaimed. "Or should I say, holy alligator! I can't set up a depo in here. This is a joke, right?"

"No," Norma said, "it's not a joke. This is Lars's office. He's used to it, so he's comfortable in here."

"Well, I'm not used to, nor am I comfortable with, looking at a tank with two alligators while reporting a depo," I asserted.

"Oh, you'll get used to them. Lars has had them for years. Their names are Ali and Able." Norma added, "I think Ali is pregnant."

"Pregnant or not, she's looking at me like her dinner just walked in," I exclaimed.

Laughing, Norma replied, "You don't need to worry. They're well fed. You can set up with the witness facing Ali and Able. You'll forget they're here, and Lars likes that they intimidate the witness."

"You want me to have my back to those hefty looking fellas? Oh, no, that's not happening. Listen, I'm billing double for reporting this depo," I declared. "Let's just call it hazardous duty pay."

"That's not a problem. We usually pay double. Reporting firms won't even take our calls," she lamented.

"I guess you thought you got yourself an alligator sucker, right? I could be an alligator stiff by the end of the day. Oh well, let me see what I can do, but I also want an appearance fee of an extra $250 if we just go through the morning, and $500 if we go all day. I'm going to have to buy a nice bottle of wine, get a massage, and call my therapist when this is over."

"Okay! Okay! I know Lars will agree to that," Norma assured me.

Thinking about it, I stated, "I'll set up over there on the far wall at the end of the desk. I'll put the witness and his counsel facing Lars sitting at his desk. I'll have a full-on view of the alligators. The witness and his counsel will have a side view, and if Ali and Able manage to get out of their tank, their first victims will be opposing counsel and his client. I'd have to dodge the action to get out of this office, but at least I'd have a fighting chance."

"Okay," Norma agreed, "but don't get too close to Lars's desk, because mid-depo he likes to pull a gun out of his drawer and place it on his desk while he looks for something in the drawer, whereupon he pulls out a bottle of whiskey and takes a slug."

"What?" I cried out, "Okay! I'm on a reality TV show, right? Where are the cameras?"

"No," Norma said, "it's really all fake, just to intimidate the witness."

"Good grief!" I grimaced. "Is there a torture rack in the closet?"

Norma hesitated, "Well…"

***

I had my equipment all set up: my DataWriter on the tripod in front of me and my laptop on a corner of Lars's desk, and the cables connecting the DataWriter to the laptop so I could see the transcript coming up in real time. I was ready to report the depo, but when the witness walked into the office and saw the alligators, he jumped a foot backward, bumping into his attorney and sending him sprawling onto the floor with his case files flying all over the place.

The witness's attorney was having difficulty standing up as he repeatedly slipped on the scattered papers. He managed to grab onto the tank and pull himself up, but in doing so, found himself a mere six inches from Ali on the other side of the glass. He screamed in terror as he lost his footing again and collapsed to the floor. He began crawling out the office door just as Lars was walking in. Lars, preoccupied with his notes, walked into the room and landed right on top of opposing counsel, who was now flattened to the floor with Lars on top of him. Opposing counsel was waving his arms and legs wildly in an attempt to crawl out of the office.

"Be still, you fool, so I can stand up," Lars hollered and managed to get to his feet.

Counsel grabbed the door frame and pulled himself up while his client sat huddled in the corner whimpering. I was laughing so hard tears were streaming down my cheeks. Lars was yelling at me, "Stop laughing. There's nothing funny about this. What's wrong with you people?"

Lars trampled over papers to get to his desk and pulled a gun out of the drawer, set it in on the desk, pulled out the whiskey bottle, and took a long drink—which, of course, only made me laugh the harder. Lars pulled another gulp from the bottle labeled "Writers' Tears."

Addressing opposing counsel, he said, "Get this mess cleaned up. We'll start the depo in fifteen minutes." He returned the gun and Writers' Tears to the drawer and stormed out of the room. Opposing counsel and I managed to get all his files back in order, while his client disappeared into the restroom.

Fifteen minutes later, Lars returned and sat down at his desk. "If you can manage to keep from laughing, could you please swear in the witness?" he snapped at me.

In a courtroom setting, the clerk swears in the witness, but in a deposition, the reporter represents the court and swears in the witness. She, or he, also calls breaks when an opportunity presents itself. For instance, the reporter wouldn't call a break in between a question and an answer, nor would she call a break if the testimony was hot and heavy. For the most part, an attorney calls for breaks before the reporter drops off her chair from exhaustion.

***

Checking my messages after the depo, I noticed one from Officer Handel, who wanted to speak to me about Jonesy's accident. I called the number he left and got Brent, Dale's childhood friend, and mine too, for that matter. Brent's father used to be a professional tennis player, so his parents traveled a lot and Brent would stay with us when they were out of town. Brent's a gangly looking guy, almost a Gomer Pyle type, who still wears the alpaca button-down-the-front golf sweaters that were popular back in the sixties. His dark brown hair is always tousled, and he commands attention with his deep brown eyes.

"Hi Brent! It's Addie. How are you doing?"

"Hey, Addie! It's a good day when we don't have too many arrests. How are you?"

"Well, I just took a depo with two alligators eyeing me."

"What?"

"Yeah," I said, "Lars has two alligators in a tank in his office. You wouldn't believe the commotion they caused this morning."

"Geez! What next?" Brent answered.

Laughing, I replied, "Therein lies the conundrum."

Brent changed the subject, "How's Dale? I haven't talked to him in weeks."

"He's in Milwaukee working as co-counsel with Uncle Bud," I replied.

"I have great memories of your mom's brother visiting the family here in Santa Monica," Brent said. "Remember when the three of us tried to teach him to surf? What a blast that was."

"He's planning on coming out next summer for another lesson," I laughed.

"Uncle Bud has had a remarkable influence on Dale," commented Brent. "I love the story about how when you guys were little tykes, back in Detroit, and Uncle Bud used to babysit for you, he'd fall asleep on the couch, studying his law books, and Dale would creep downstairs, cuddle up to him and pretend he was reading and understanding the law. It was the beginning of a budding career."

"And remember how much fun we had when Dale would make us play courtroom?" I reminisced. "He was the attorney, I was the judge, and you were the jury."

"Even as a kid, he gave incredible closing arguments," Bent remarked.

"That Dale not only passed the Bar in California, but Wisconsin, Washington, and New York as well, is a major achievement," I added. "At any rate, he's having a great time working with Uncle Bud."

That started me thinking about how much Dale and Uncle Bud look alike, especially since Dale started wearing glasses. Uncle Bud is about five-eleven. Dale is six-one. They both have the beloved, smoky-blue eyes so celebrated in our family. Female jurors have swooned over both men. Uncle Bud is a runner and lanky. Dale works out with weights and he surfs, so he's solid. They both dress flawlessly in traditional lawyerly suits. Uncle Bud's hair has turned gray, but Dale still has sandy-blond hair with just a hint of Mom's natural curl.

Brent brought me out of my woolgathering. "It must be nice to be a rich and sought-   after attorney, jet-setting all over the world. Sometimes I regret dropping out of law school, but I love being a cop. Most days, that is."

"I'm proud of the two of you," I said. "You're doing what you love and making a difference. On another note, I had a message from Officer Handel.

He wants me to call him. I don't know him. Is he new? Having lived in this town for forty-two years, I thought I knew everyone."

"Yeah, actually, he is new," Brent said, "right out of the academy. He's Newsome's partner. You remember Newsome. Dale and I played on a Pony League team with him."

"Yes, of course. It's all coming back to me. I guess I should speak to him."

"He's not in right now, but I can tell you what he wants to talk to you about," Brent stated. "A pair of sunglasses looking suspiciously like yours were found at the scene of the crime of Jones's death."

"What?" I retorted. "Scene of the crime? What happened? I thought it was an accident."

Brent said, "We discovered that the brakes were tampered with. Jones lost control of the car and went over the cliff."

"Holy mackerel!" I blurted. "That's horrible. Who would want to kill Jonesy? He was so kind and such a gentleman."

"That's what we're going to find out," Brent assured me.

"What a shock!" I declared. "I'm pretty sure those are my sunglasses, though. I wondered where I'd left them. Jonesy took me for a ride in his Maserati just before we both headed over the canyon for home."

"Well, that explains how your sunglasses were found at the scene," Brent said. "We found them and some other items that were blown out of the car when it exploded. Did you notice anything unusual about the car when he took you for a ride?"

"No, we just more or less went around the block. There was a lot of traffic. Jonesy left ahead of me after dropping me back at the parking garage. I had to wait for my car to be brought up, but I was close behind him. Come to think of it, it took about ten minutes for my car to come up, yet I was right behind Jonesy. He must have returned to his office for something."

"Were his case files in the car when you went for a drive?" Brent asked. "We found burned fragments of loose case files at the scene."

"No," I answered, "I didn't see any files. That must be what he went back up to the office to get."

"Yeah, maybe," Brent said thoughtfully. "Well, thanks, Addie. I'll let Handel know I spoke to you."

"Okay," I said. "I'll see you at Dale's Halloween party, if not sooner. I can hardly wait. I love the old Kniss house on the beach—such good memories of playing volleyball, surfing, and beach parties."

Brent laughed, "Oh, yes! Those were the days, Gidget!"

***

The depo only went a couple of hours, so I took Norma up on the offer of lunch. As I approached the front door of Eddie's, the hottest new lunch place in the area, I noticed the blinking orange lights and pumpkins scattered about, giving it a festive look. I walked in and saw that Norma had secured a table. I was glad she did, because the place was packed.

"Hi, Norma! How are you doing?"

"I'm good for my condition," she replied. "My baby is due in a few weeks. I feel like a beached whale, and the baby kicks all night, so I'm not getting much sleep. I'm tired all the time. But it's only a few more weeks, and then I will have a precious bundle of joy. It's all very exciting."

"It was one of the most exciting times in my life, too," I said. "That was twenty-seven years ago. I had a management job with the phone company. In those days, the job commanded an extremely professional maternity wardrobe, which I loved."

"And I bet you looked adorable in your maternity clothes with your beautiful bobbed, blonde hair and those deep blue eyes and trim figure," Norma said. "How tall are you, about five-two?"

"Exactly," I replied. "And I'm an avid runner, which helps burn unwanted calories and relieve stress."

"I've fought weight issues all my life," Norma admitted.

"Haven't we all," I agreed. "My mom was a ninety-seven-pound Vogue model. She didn't have weight issues, though. She was just a fussy eater and an atrocious cook. I think the important thing is to live a healthy lifestyle."

"Me too," Norma said. "Of course, now I'm into my health more than ever."

"Norma, you are simply glowing. Will you hire a temp to take your place while you're on maternity leave?"

"No, Lars's daughter will come in to run the office for a month."

"I bet your husband is excited," I commented.

"My ex-husband," Norma stated. "We were in the throes of a divorce when I realized I was pregnant, but there was no going back with that cheating jerk. He got his assistant pregnant, and she's expecting a baby about the same time I am."

"Yikes! That's got to be so hard on you," I exclaimed.

"It was at first," she agreed, "but I'd been through so much craziness with him, I was ready to get out of the relationship. And I met someone else, so everything happens for the best."

"Sometimes it does," I assured her.

***

After lunch, I ran some errands and arrived home in time to send today's job to Patrice, change clothes, collect Mother, and head down to the Music Center for an opera gala. Dale and I have season tickets, but I'm taking Mom since he's out of town. She isn't big on opera, but she loves social events. She especially enjoys wearing all her beautiful gowns.

Mom was a Vogue model in the late '30s and early '40s and kept many of her clothes from that era. At seventy-two, Mom is still the epitome of a model. She stands erect and walks like she's on the runway. Her naturally curly hair is kept dyed a chestnut brown and cut short with loose curls. I inherited my beautiful, smoky-blue eyes from her. I often wish we were the same size so I could wear her lovely gowns, but she's five-five and a hundred and ten pounds. I'm five-two and a hundred and ten pounds. My sister, Little Missy, could wear them, but she wouldn't be caught dead in anything that wasn't in fashion at the very moment. She literally throws out last year's fashions, while I still have some clothing from my high school days.

On the drive to the Music Center, I listened to Mom chatter about the latest Santa Monica gossip. Gossip is her newfound career.

"Addie, did you know that Handel is the Newsome boy's partner? You know, my father had a gay friend. He was an oncologist like my dad. Nicest guy. He came to all my parents' cocktail parties. He'd bring gentlemen friends. He finally settled on Robert. They were together for forty-seven years. Isn't that lovely?"

"Yes, Mom, it is."

"Honey, did you know that Larceny's expert doctor never examined me nor gave me any tests regarding Missy's lawsuit? He spent ten minutes with me and billed for all sorts of tests and exams. I think he's a cheater."

"Really?" I voiced. "No, I didn't know that. He's Lars's expert doc on the Medi-Cal case, too. From some of the exhibits I've seen, I was pretty sure he was at least padding his bills. I wonder if

Jonesy knew, and if that could be what got him killed."

Chapter 4: A Man in Black

Still Thursday

"Champagne, ma'am?"

"Oh, yes, thank you," Mom said, taking one for me as well.

"Oh my gosh, Mom! There's Dixie. I haven't seen her in so long." Dixie caught my eye and rushed over to us. "Hi, Dixie!"

"Hey, Addie. Hello, Vesta. You look charmin' tonight as always, Vesta. I'm in total envy of your amazing wardrobe. If I were taller and thinner, I'd be beggin' to borrow," she said. Dixie is about five-three and super lean, but quite strong. She has thinning, ash-blonde hair and brilliant brown eyes.

Mom loves it when people notice her exquisite gowns. "Thank you, Dixie. You look quite stunning tonight as well."

Dixie began her career as a fashion designer. When she and Mom got to talking about '40s fashion, the conversation could go on for hours, but Mom saw one of her tennis buddies and excused herself.

"I heard that you got a condo downtown here," I said. "How do you like the best of two fab cities, all the excitement of downtown theaters and restaurants, and then the laid-back, sandy beach life?"

"Oh, Addie, I love it, and I adore my condo. It's right across from the Los Angeles Athletic Club. They have a great bar, and their restaurant is quite good, too. I'm workin' as a personal trainer there. And as for my side biz, I got an offer I couldn't refuse. The guy bought the condo for me, and paid cash. I couldn't believe it. But he's a difficult one. He likes to play peeky, you know, have someone watch him with the girls, and he likes lots of different girls at all hours of the day and night. I'm havin' a hard time comin' up with new gals. I don't suppose I could interest you." Dixie's not-so-successful fashion design business soon turned into one of the most popular and pricey escort services in Southern California.

"Oh, no," I quickly cut in.

"I used to pay gals a hundred bucks an hour for peekin'," she continued. "This guy pays a grand an hour just for peekin'. He's got to be a multi-millionaire. Oops! There he is. Walk over here with me. I gotta pretend I don't know him. He's a very pious Jew"—she laughed—"what a scam! He's a sex addict. I wish we could bottle his sex drive. What guy wouldn't pay for it, huh?"

"That's Larceny," I whispered. "The guy in the tux with the beard and yarmulke; is he the one you're talking about?"

"Yes. He's an attorney," Dixie said. "He likes to have clients—that's what he calls the girls— come to his office during the day. He enjoys the thrill of maybe gettin' caught. Did you know he keeps two alligators in his office? The girls are scared to death of them. We charge a lot more for full-on sex in his office."

"Unbelievable," I sputtered. "I do know about the alligators. I did a depo in his office this morning. Gave me the creeps, but I raised the rent, so to speak, and got paid twice as much as normal."

Dixie said, "Yep, that's what we do, too. Listen, darlin', I've gotta go. Larceny wants a little entertainment after the benefit. Let's get together for drinks at the Athletic Club. Check your calendar and call me."

"Okay," I replied. "See you soon."

***

I caught up to Mom, and we wandered around, chatting with old friends and new. It was after 11:00 when we arrived home. I walked Mom to the cottage and headed for my front door,

where I found a note from Jaime reading, "Knock on my door as soon as you get home, no matter how late it is. J." I wondered what this was about. Suddenly, his door swung open.

"Addie, come in here quickly. Let's go into the living room. I know it's late, but Chris has a pitcher of martinis, and I think you'll need one."

I followed him down the long hall into the living room, asking, "What's happened?"

"Well, you just missed all the excitement. Thank goodness you installed this fantastic security system last year. I know you were upset when Little Missy threatened to put a hitman on you, and we really did think you'd lost your marbles, but it paid for itself tonight. Chris and I were sitting here reading quietly by the fireplace when we suddenly heard a banging on the side of the house. We looked at each other questioningly. Then we heard something bouncing against the wall and ran to the back room to look out the window, thinking it was the wind blowing something around. Right then, the bells and whistles went off. I have to tell you, that's the most awful screeching noise, worse than Florence Foster Jenkins singing opera. We ran outside to investigate, but we couldn't see much. The security light was out. I'm sorry; I keep forgetting to replace that.

"The next thing we knew, Chris was on the ground, having been hit on the back of the head by a falling ladder. I was too concerned about Chris to see anything else, but Helen, from next door, saw a man running toward a utility vehicle. He tripped on her inflatable light-up pumpkin reaper but managed to get to his van and take off before she could get a license number or any identifying info."

That's when I noticed Chris holding an icepack to his head and sipping a martini. "Oh, Chris, I'm so sorry you got hit on the head. Are you okay?"

"I'm good. No worries, love. But what an odd thing to happen. In this neighborhood? A guy dressed in black with a utility truck and a ladder this late at night? Very odd."

"Yeah, weird!" continued Jaime, "Because they're so close, the police showed up around the same time the security company called. We made a police report, but what a botched-up robbery attempt. Someone must have found out about all those diamonds you have hidden upstairs."

"Oh, for goodness' sake," I declared. "I know you're teasing, but I also know you know I love my jewelry, and I keep it in a well-hidden safe. Plus, it's insured, but the sentimental value of my grandma's diamonds and sapphires could never be replaced. This is a very wealthy neighborhood, though. It would make more sense to rob a house with luxury cars, chauffeurs, and chefs coming and going. After all, everyone knows I only live here because I inherited the property, and it's paid for."

"Well," Jaime went on, "since there was no harm, no foul, I doubt the police will be fingerprinting or doing any further investigation—unless you want to see if you can get Brent on it."

"No," I replied. "It was probably just some random guy deciding to take a stab at robbing one of the neighborhood homes. Let's get a good night's sleep and look outside in the morning. Love you guys. Thanks for the martini, Chris."

Jaime and Chris may laugh at me for our sophisticated security system, but I sleep well, knowing all the bells and whistles will go off if anyone attempts to break in.

A guy dressed in black with a utility van. Was it just a random act of attempted robbery? Who'd want to come after me?

Chapter 5: Oneg Shabbat

Friday, October 4, 1996

I was still wondering why someone would pick this house to rob. Maybe because we're the least expensive-looking house in the neighborhood, and our security system isn't as noticeable as others. We don't have big gates or a security guard.

On a more important note, though, who could have wanted Jonesy dead? Baxter certainly announced that he wanted to kill him. Who else had motive, means, and opportunity? Everyone knew Lars was a crook, although no one had proven it yet. Maybe Jonesy came across evidence that would expose Lars, and Lars altered the brake system on Jonesy's car. However, I couldn't see Lars getting his hands dirty. But then, if Jonesy had evidence linking Lars to crime, surely Norma would know about it. She sees almost every document that goes through the office. Would Norma have the motive to kill Jonesy? I do remember her leaving the office early that day.

The ringing of my phone brought me out of my thoughts. "Hi, Brent! What's up?"

"You haven't picked up your sunglasses yet."

"Oh, geez! Thank you. I forgot all about them." I confessed. "Hey, if you're coming to Friday night services tonight, would you bring them with you?

Mom and I are going. She adores Cantor Cohen, and he'll be leading the service tonight."

"Yes, I'll be bringing my mom, too. And I think Newsome and Handel will also be going, so you'll be able to meet Officer Handel."

"Wonderful! And I always enjoy seeing your mom. I'd better get off to my job. See you later."

"Bye, bye, Gidget."

Little did I know how many things could become clear at Oneg Shabbat following Friday night services.

***

The peace of Friday night service melted away all the accumulated tension of the week. Cantor Cohen has a special place in my heart. He officiated at my bat mitzvah and then again at Kat's. Our small congregation cannot always afford a rabbi, so Cantor Cohen has stepped in through the years. His announcements for the week included that the funeral for Jonesy would be held on Sunday at 1:00, with a celebration of life reception following. After the service, we filed into the all-purpose room for the Oneg, which consists of greeting friends and drinking coffee, lemonade, or wine, and eating cookies. Mom and I chatted with Cantor Cohen, and Newsome joined us. Cantor Cohen greeted him and then excused himself.

Newsome turned to us. "Addie and Vesta, I'd like you to meet my partner, Henry Handel."

"Henry," I said, "it's nice to finally meet you."

Mom piped in. "It's an honor. Your mother-in-law and I play bridge together, so I've heard wonderful things about you. She says you're quite a chef and that the fifties' casseroles are your specialty." She was looking at Handel but gave me a side glance and a little smirk. Translation: *see how popular fifties' casseroles are.*

Mom was engaged in deep conversation with Handel when Brent joined us. "Brent, thank you for remembering my sunglasses," I said. "These prescription glasses are expensive to replace. Say, I was wondering if you knew about Baxter. He was our witness at the depo the day of Jonesy's death. He threatened to kill Jonesy. In fact, he jumped across the table and got Jonesy in a stranglehold. Tommy, the security officer, had to pull him off Jonesy and handcuff him. Just another amusing day in the life of a court reporter."

"Actually, we spoke to Norma," he assured me, "and she did mention that little scene. As it turns out, Tommy held Baxter in security for several hours. He wanted to be sure Jonesy didn't want to file charges. Baxter's attorney was fed up with his client, so he took off."

"So, Baxter wouldn't have had the opportunity to alter the brakes on Jonesy's car," I concluded. "What about Norma? Have you checked her out?"

"Norma? Why?" Brent asked.

"Oh, I don't know," I confessed. "I'm reaching, but she did leave the office early that day."

"I can't picture a very pregnant Norma being an auto mechanic," Brent said.

"Well, that's a bit sexist, if I do say. Remember, I'm the gal who helped Dale put his Jaguar coupe back together before Dad could find out he'd taken it apart."

"You've got a point," Brent admitted, "but we're looking at Lars. If Jonesy did have evidence that could incriminate him, Lars would certainly want to protect his assets."

"By the way," I said, "did you know that Lars is a sex addict?"

"No! Really?"

"Yes. I ran into a friend at an opera gala the other night, and she told me all about it. Apparently, Lars throws a lot of money around on women, condos, theater tickets, not to mention he pays top dollar for sex, and lots of it. If he's trying to protect his assets, that's motive for criminal behavior."

"It sure is," Brent agreed, "and, we'll look into it."

"I'd better collect my mom and head home," I said.

"Okay. Thanks, Gidget," Brent smiled. "See you soon."

Mom was walking toward me as I turned around. "Hey Mom, I'm just going to use the restroom before we leave. I'll be right back."

As I approached the restroom, I heard someone crying and stumbling over her words. I hesitated going in because I didn't want to embarrass whoever it was. Then I recognized Mrs. L., Lars's wife, wringing her hands as she spoke to the rabbi's wife.

"Lars is so cruel. He told me he only married me for my family money. He said it's all my fault he sleeps with other women because I'm boring in bed. I hate to say it in shul and on shabbat, but I could kill the son of a bitch. He throws his affairs in my face. He says I'm fat and ugly."

I decided I could wait till we got home to use the restroom.

Chapter 6: Decorations and Campbell's Soup

Saturday, October 5, 1996

I decided to get out my Halloween decorations, but I needed coffee first. While I waited for the espresso machine to warm up, I began to think about Mrs. L. So, she knew about Lars's affairs and spending habits. How hurt she must be. Could she be hurt enough to commit murder? She said she could kill Lars, but why on earth would she kill Jonesy? Maybe because she has a financial stake in the law firm, and if Jonesy threatened her income, that might be a motive to kill.

I gulped down my espresso, put on some work clothes, and started hauling boxes up from the garage. Mom used to enjoy doing ceramics and made beautiful Halloween decorations for me. One of my favorites is a lamp in the shape of a ghost holding a pumpkin, and when it's turned on, it lights up the ghost's face. It took me all morning to get everything in place. Then I went over to see if Mom wanted me to help her get out her decorations, but Jaime was already there giving her a hand. I opened a box and began working along with them.

Although Mom is legally blind, she can still handle most activities of daily living and see well enough to live alone with some guidance and caution. She loves working in the garden, but sometimes pulls up flowers rather than weeds or cuts off live branches instead of the dead ones. Mom desperately wants to be independent, so I manage that wherever possible. Instead of washing her clothes, I noticed she rinsed them because she couldn't read the buttons on the washer, so I put big colored dots on the various cycles. After she burned up four irons, I told her how relaxing I found ironing, yet I didn't generate much, so would she mind very much if I did some of hers. More important, Mom loves to cook, so we have color-coded stove knobs and oven temperatures.

Mom used to be the world's worst cook. Being a ninety-seven-pound Vogue model did not lend itself to the kitchen. When Dale and Missy and I were little, she made the same meals each day of the week, and they were ghastly. As she got older, though, she found that she enjoyed cooking and entertaining. My mother loves throwing parties, and her cooking skills have improved—although, she's somewhat stuck in the fifties Campbell's soup casserole era, maybe because modeling for Campbell's soup ads as a kid kicked off her modeling career.

I started hauling Mom's empty Halloween boxes back to the garage. Mom followed me, carrying a few as well.

"Addie," she said, "I forgot to tell you that I found a knit black cap in the garden yesterday. Do you think it could belong to the guy who tried robbing us the other night?"

"Gosh, I don't know. Maybe. Our garden is fenced and gated, so I don't think anyone else would have come in uninvited," I speculated. "What did you do with it?"

"I picked it up with my fingertips and bagged it," she said. "I watch *Prime Suspect*, you know. Helen Mirren is one of my favorite actresses. She reminds me of you. You're both so pretty and smart."

"Oh, Mom, that's so sweet. Thank you." I gave her a big hug. "I doubt that an attempted robbery warrants DNA testing, but I'll give it to Brent."

Chapter 7: A Funeral
Sunday, October 6, 1996

I had a lot of proofing to do before leaving for Jonesy's funeral, so I skipped my run in favor of working. It was a bright, sunny morning with a hint of chillness in the air. I put on a sweatshirt and settled in the garden with coffee and transcripts. I finished just before eleven, sent the corrected transcripts to Patrice, and hopped in the shower.

I chose a black Chanel suit out of my closet, matched it with sensible black high heels, purse, and gloves. I donned a Louise Green wide-brimmed black hat with black gossamer band, and I got downstairs at 11:30 a.m. on the dot. In Los Angeles, you have to allow plenty of time to get anywhere. Chris, Mom, Jaime, and I hopped in Chris's 1994 Jaguar. We were going in style.

Mom and Jaime had known Jonesy quite well from Missy's failed lawsuit. Chris decided to come along for the ride. We're from the generation where our grandparents took us on Sunday afternoon drives. We arrived at Forest Lawn Cemetery at 12:30 p.m., and Chris dropped us all off and went to find parking. We walked into the prayer hall, also known as an ohel, and located seats near the front. Jonesy's parents sat in the front row. They came from San Francisco and carried the patina of old money and good breeding—thus Jonesy's law school graduation gift of a Maserati.

Jonesy had been an only child. How much pain his parents must be suffering. Jonesy was single. He dated some, but it's difficult for an attorney coming out of law school and joining a firm to have time for social activities. Their hours are long. They're often seen burning the midnight oil. That's why law firms support gyms and restaurants in their buildings. Some have even begun introducing childcare.

In other pews, I noticed several young people, most likely Jonesy's collegemates. Chris joined us at our seats. The rabbi walked up to the lectern and began speaking of Jonesy. He was raised in San Francisco, went to Stanford for his undergraduate work, and graduated from Harvard Law School. A brilliant young man with his whole life ahead of him. Tears slowly made their way down our cheeks. Boxes of Kleenex were passed around.

When the rabbi finished speaking, we all filed out to the graveside. Chairs had been set up. We found some seats in a middle row. I noticed a well-built gentleman of medium height and graying hair, standing in the back. His hands were clasped in front of him, and he stared straight ahead. He looked so familiar. I stood up and walked toward him to get a better look. Gabe?

He turned abruptly and began walking toward the buildings. From behind, he looked like Gabe, except that he had a slight limp.

"Gabe? Gabe! Whoever you are, please wait. I just want to speak to you for a moment," I shouted.

When he walked into the building, I jogged to the door and pulled it open, but I didn't see anyone.

I went down the hall, opening doors and peering inside empty rooms. I called, "Gabe?" But I got no answer. I searched the building as best I could. He was nowhere. I sat down on a bench. Tears threatened to erupt. Was I imagining that I saw Gabe? Is he simply on my mind due to Jonesy's violent death, a burning car, a burning building, my dreams?

The door opened and Brent sprinted down the hallway and sat down next to me. "Addie, what's going on? Are you alright? I saw you race into the building, and I came after you."

"I thought I saw Gabe," I ventured. "I darted into the building, but he was gone. Brent, am I going crazy?"

"No, you're not going crazy," Brent assured me. "Gabe's body was never recovered. You didn't have closure. You want him to be alive. Trust me, Addie, if Gabe were alive, he would find you."

I was trying hard not to cry. "Maybe he survived and has amnesia. He doesn't know who he is."

"The CIA worked on that theory," Brent reminded me. "If anyone can be found, the CIA will find him or her. He never turned up. I'm sorry, Ads. Grief never goes away, it just changes over time."

"I know, but I can't let go of hope. If I did, I'd have to let go of him."

Brent bundled me in his arms and held me tight. "Are you okay to go back and join the others?" he finally asked.

"Yes. Thank you. I don't want to worry Mom and Chris and Jaime. Let's just tell them I was desperate for a martini." We laughed and walked back outside.

***

We arrived home about 4:30 p.m. and decided to meet in the garden for cocktails at 5:00 p.m. I changed into some warm, comfy black lounging pants and an orange and black striped shirt; checked my messages; made a batch of martinis; grabbed glasses and my favorite dark green, long-sleeved, cable-knit sweater that Mom had made for me when I was in high school.

The evening air was chilly, so we turned on the outdoor heaters and the fire pit. I took a wool lap blanket from the pile we kept there. The garden glowed in the firelight. I felt safe, happy, and so very fortunate to be with my family and friends. I lived in the town I grew up in, in my family home. I was financially secure due to my parents' long-term planning, generosity, and my own hard work. What more could I ask for?

Gabe.

"Earth to Addie, come in."

I was pulled from my musing by Chris's gentle probing. I smiled at him. "I was counting my blessings."

Chris questioned, "As in the song from my favorite all-time movie, *White Christmas*, which we'll be watching in no time at all? The holidays are creeping up on us."

At that moment, my cell phone sang, "Teacher's Pet," my ring tone for Kat. "Hello, my beautiful baby girl. How are you doing?"

"I'm great, Mom," she said.

"Can I put you on speaker?" I asked. "I'm in the garden with Grandma, Chris, and Jaime."

"Of course. Hi everyone!"

There was a chorus of exclamations, "Hi, Kat! How are you?"

"I'm good. I love my new home in LO. That's what the locals call Lake Oswego. I'm right near the water, and there are amazing running trails all around. My teaching position is a dream come true, and the campus is absolutely stunning with its brick buildings laced with ivy and its charming English gardens. Sometimes, I pinch myself just to make sure I'm not dreaming. Guess what I did today? Oh, you'll never guess, so I'll tell you. I got a puppy. She's a rescue—mostly lab, I think—and cute, cute, cute. Aren't you, sweet little girl? Say hi to Grandma."

Great Scott! Now I'm grandmother to a dog. Oh, well. "Okay. That's it. I must come up next weekend and meet my new grand-dog before she grows up."

"Wonderful!" Kat declared. "Grandad should be here, too. He's wrapping up his consultation work on the aviation museum in New Zealand, and he's dying to see my new digs and the campus. I have four bedrooms plus a rumpus room, so there's plenty of space."

"I'll see what sort of flight I can get, and I'll bring Grandma, too," I said.

"That would be wonderful. I miss all of you," Kat said. "How's everybody doing?"

"Well, today was a bit of a downer. We went to Jonesy's funeral."

"I remember Jonesy from Aunt Missy's ridiculous lawsuit. What a sad way to spend a beautiful Sunday."

"Yes, it was, but we're rallying around with martinis," I admitted.

"Oh, you guys and your martinis." Kat's limits are an occasional glass of wine or a margarita. "I'd better let you go. I need to take Puppy outside."

"Okay, honey, but tell me, what will you name your new darling?" I asked.

"I'm thinking about that. Names are important. For now, she's Puppy," Kat announced.

"Actually, that's quite a cute name. I'll call you when I have a flight arranged."

"Okay. Bye Mom. Love you."

"Love you, too, sweetie."

My daughter is gorgeous beyond belief. She's five-five, with long blonde hair that she highlights. She has the family's smoky blue eyes. Kat's also a runner, works out with weights, and does spin-cycle classes both for fun and to keep in shape.

Chris had gone inside and come out with steaks to put on the barbecue. We decided rather than eat dinner in the garden, we'd eat on Chris and Jaime's elegant, closed-in patio overlooking the garden. Mom brought over her infamous sponge cake.

She'd used food coloring to make it orange and topped it with ghosts and goblins, practicing on us for the upcoming American Association of University Women (AAUW) Halloween bake sale. I contributed a delicious pinot noir I'd picked up at the International Pinot Noir Celebration in McMinnville, Oregon, last summer. While we drank the superb wine, we reminisced about vacations spent in Ashland.

Dale and I, and sometimes Missy, grew up on Ashland summers. Ashland, Oregon, is the home of the Oregon Shakespeare Festival and so much more.

Back in the late '30s, Uncle Bill made a trip along the Oregon Coast and, being a Bard aficionado, he visited Ashland and fell in love. During World War II, he met my Auntie Bev. He was a wounded soldier, and she was the nurse who brought him back to life. He regaled her with stories of Shakespeare and Ashland. After the war, they purchased a beautiful Victorian home on Main Street and turned it into a bed and breakfast inn. To honor Auntie Bev, Uncle Bill named it Nightingales, after Florence Nightingale, the founder of modern nursing.

Dale and I used to sleep in the attic that Uncle Bill fixed up for us. When Missy was around, we'd scare her to death with stunts and stories about the ghost of Grandma Russell, the woman who built the house in 1901. Missy threw fits and ran screaming down the stairs.

Before performances, and during the intermissions in the outdoor Elizabethan theatre, Dale and I would run up and down the aisles, pretending we were Shakespearean actors. On a few occasions an actor would invite us onto the stage, whereupon Dale got his drama practice for the courtroom, and I became enthralled with Shakespeare and literature.

The dinner conversation eventually turned to depositions and scheduling. Mom excused herself, "I'm going to go curl up on my sofa with Janet Dawson's latest book, *A Credible Threat*." She walked across the garden to her cottage while I helped Jaime and Chris clear dishes and stack them in the dishwasher. Then I said goodnight and headed upstairs to watch an American Movie Classics movie I'd recorded on my VCR. It was the perfect ending to a lovely weekend—other than, of course, Jonesy's funeral and the mystery man.

Chapter 8: Padded Bills

Monday, October 7, 1996

I ran down to Palisades Park and along the ocean. There's nothing like the brisk ocean air first thing in the morning. The pungent smell of strong coffee and sweet pastries lured me to my favorite vendor. I bought lattes overflowing with delicious foam, and almond poppy seed muffins still warm from the oven. My hands were full, so I walked back home. After dropping a latte and muffin off to Mom and Jaime, I savored mine while packing my equipment before heading back to Lars's office for the expert doctor's depo in the Medi-Cal case. I took a hot shower and dressed in a periwinkle wool tweed suit and a pale blue silk blouse with a bow-tie collar. I loaded my equipment into my new 1996 red-and-black Mini Cooper and headed into the traffic.

***

"Do you solemnly swear or affirm that the testimony you are about to give in the proceedings before us shall be the truth, the whole truth, and nothing but the truth?"

"I won't swear, but I will affirm," bellowed Lars's rather large expert doc. I instantly disliked this man. He was cocky, and he was smoking a cigar.

I admonished him with my standard cigar, cigarette pronouncement: "Doctor, I'm terribly sorry, but I'm allergic to tobacco smoke. You can either put out your cigar, or we can adjourn while we see if another reporter is available today."

Expert Doc jumped in, "Well, let's adjourn then."

Lars instantly spoke up, "No, no, he'll put it out."

Expert Doc grudgingly put out the cigar but continued chewing on it.

Opposing Counsel Appel began the questioning with preliminaries. "Can you state your full name for the record, please."

With the unlit cigar in his mouth, Expert Doc mumbled something indistinguishable.

Again, I admonished, "Doctor, it's important that we get an accurate record of the testimony you're giving here today. To facilitate that, will you please remove the cigar from your mouth so we can understand what you're saying?"

Expert Doc complied and the deposition continued. I liked Counsel Appel. He took a slow and methodical deposition. There were a lot of documents to enter into evidence, and he stopped and had me mark each one, rather than throw them on the table into a tossed-together mess that we'd have to figure out later.

At lunchtime, I went back into the transcript on my laptop and entered a brief description of each document. There were a lot of patient records and numerous bills. I was shocked at how high the doctors' bills were. Although I faint at the sight of blood, I now thought I should have followed in my grandfather's footsteps, persevered and gone to medical school. The charges for patient care really added up.

I was pulled out of my reverie with the arrival of the delivery girl bringing my tuna salad from the deli downstairs. I like to work through my lunch hour and breaks because then I don't have so much work to do when I return home at night.

Everyone drifted back in about 1:30. We went back on the record and the questioning continued. It was so boring, I was in danger of falling asleep, so I called a break at three o'clock and took a little stroll around the office to wake myself up. I grabbed a Mars bar from the bowl of Halloween candy on Norma's desk and spotted some wedding and baby planning books along with a stack of documents entered into evidence at Jonesy's last depo. I wondered why she had the docs. We bind them in the deposition transcript, and they're virtually impossible to remove. Maybe they're copies. It's hard to tell without walking around the desk and examining them, and I sure didn't want to get caught snooping. Jonesy knew Lars was cheating. Could there be evidence in those documents? Wait! Wedding planning books? Is Norma getting married? To whom?

We reconvened the depo at 3:30, and the questioning got heated. Expert Doc was quite literally sweating and mopping his forehead with the monogrammed hanky in his dark gray, tailor-made suit jacket pocket. And, in between the question and answer, he was vigorously chewing on that darn cigar. I typed in:

Question: These bills appear to be quite high.

Lars: Objection, that's not a question.

Question: What is your normal rate for examining a Medi-Cal patient?

Answer: $500 an hour.

Question: If my math is correct, these bills indicate $750 an hour.

Lars: Objection, that's not a question.

Question: Is that right?

Answer: I— er— I don't know. I—er— I'd have to do some math.

Question: Well, here you go. Here's a calculator, pen, paper, and the bills, which we'll mark into evidence as Plaintiff's Exhibit 21. Take your time. We'll adjourn while you work on that. Let me know when you're ready to resume.

I typed in, "Off the record at 4:09 p.m."

***

Opposing counsel walked out into the hall to make some calls. I strolled into the reception area to stretch and clear my head. I checked my messages and returned a call from my dentist reminding me that I was due for a cleaning.

As I walked back into the conference room, I passed Lars's office and heard Expert Doc yelling at him.

"I'm not going to do this anymore. I want out. I'm tired of living in fear of getting caught."

"Keep your voice down. I don't want Norma to hear you," Lars said, raising his voice to be heard over Expert Doc.

Their voices became mumbled, so I went into the conference room to do a little work, but I couldn't stop thinking about what the doc had said about not wanting to do this anymore.

What didn't he want to do? What did he want out of? And why did he want out?

Opposing counsel returned, and, a few minutes later, Lars did as well. We went back on the record. Addressing the witness, I said, and typed into the record, "I just want to remind you that you're still under oath." When I think a witness might be prevaricating, I like to remind them that they are testifying under oath.

"We're adjourning the depo for today. My client is ill and unable to continue," Lars spoke up before opposing counsel could ask a question.

When I got home, I went right to work on getting the transcript out to Patrice. I took a closer look at the exhibits. I was familiar with doctor bills and Medi-Cal-related expenses because Mom had been on a ventilator in a subacute nursing facility for about six months following a bout with shingles, pneumonia, and staph infections. These records did have a lot of hidden expenses; unnecessary procedures, some of which may not have been done; and what appeared to be very high billing rates for doctors' visits and consultations.

It would appear that Lars and Expert Doc were scamming the government and collecting a lot of money not legally due them. Had Jonesy discovered this illegal activity? If so, did he confront them?

Chapter 9: Too Good to Be True

Tuesday, October 8, 1996

Jaime called while I was making coffee. "Hey, darlin', whatcha doin'?"

"Oh, no, I see it coming. I can tell from the tone of your voice. What is it? An emergency in Zimbabwe? You're flying me out tonight?"

"Close. Remember that Dreyer's case you worked on about ten years ago?"

"Don't tell me someone needs an expert in ice cream. We'll have to call Kat." My daughter is a connoisseur of high-end ice creams.

"No. No. Maritime reporting. They asked for you."

"What firm?" I asked.

"Never heard of them—Smiley, Skunk & Bimball in Atlanta. Friends of yours?"

"Atlanta? I wonder how they got my name."

"Probably that Guide to Expert Reporters you put your name in last year."

"Could be. Anyway, there's no way I'm going to Atlanta. They must know someone local."

"Well, herein lies the catch. It's ten dollars a page, six copies at five dollars a page, rough drafts daily at double the usual rate. All expenses paid, and they're putting you up at the Hotel Indigo. You'll have a first-class, round-trip ticket; and they'll provide a rental car, a Beemer, which you can pick up at the airport. They've got fifteen witnesses, and they've scheduled ten days of depositions. I know you report because you love it, but, girl, this is your retirement job."

"Jumpin' jupiters! I'm in. Although, it does sound too good to be true."

***

I had a depo scheduled to begin at ten o'clock down in the Wilshire District. The traffic was miserable coming and going. It was an interesting case, though. A fourteen-year-old actress, under the thumb of her mother, was petitioning to have her sister as her guardian. At first, I felt sorry for the mother, but the testimony portrayed a mother who abused her daughter and stole her money. I typed into the record:

Question: Can you tell us a little bit about your relationship with your mother?

Answer: She tells me I'm fat. She doesn't allow me to eat—not much, anyway. I'm always hungry. When she sees me sneaking food, she makes me throw up, so I don't gain weight. She refuses to give me any spending money. She says we have too many expenses.

The actress looked extremely frail, physically and emotionally. While she wasn't exactly skin and bones, she was very close to it. Her sister appeared to be in her twenties and sat next to the actress, holding her hand. Saddened, I began thinking of my own family. What a dysfunctional cast of characters. My parents never abused us, but when

Dad found out Missy was seven months pregnant in her junior year of high school, he insisted she give the baby up for adoption. She refused, and Dad was furious. They butted heads until she finally ran off and got married so she could keep the baby. Dad hasn't spoken to Missy since, nor has he ever acknowledged her daughters, Luna and Sunbeam. In his mind's eye, his only grandchild is Kat. He adores her. My sister's anger portrays her devastation over the abandonment of her father. And my nieces have missed an important relationship in their lives.

Thank goodness the depo only went till three o'clock. It was depressing, and I needed to pack for my trip to Atlanta. I did, though, decide I should call my dad. Traffic was horrible, so I didn't arrive home until 5:15. I sent my depo to Patrice and called Dad. He answered on the first ring.

"How's my princess?"

"I'm good. Busy as always." I was still Dad's princess, and Dale was still his pal. "How's it going over there at the museum?"

"It's going great. I love this sort of work. The history of aviation is as important as the future. I wanted to see Kat this coming weekend and hoped you would meet me there, but it looks like this project will delay me for another week or two."

"That's fine. There's so much going on here, I wouldn't be able to get up to Portland for a while. Jonesy was murdered. Someone altered his brakes, and he went over Topanga Canyon."

"Holy smokes!" exclaimed Dad. "I only met him a few times, but that's shocking. Such a nice young man with his whole life ahead of him. Why would anyone want him dead?"

"That's what we're all wondering. I'm also going to Atlanta for a week of depositions," I added, "and I plan on contacting Missy. It's time this nonsense of not speaking stopped. It wouldn't hurt you to contact Missy either, Dad. You're not only missing out on her life but the lives of Luna and Sunbeam as well."

"From what I hear, I'm only missing out on a lot of headaches," Dad countered.

"Ah! So, you are keeping up with what's going on with Missy and her girls?"

"Okay, I admit I occasionally have Valentin check up on them for me. Missy just won't grow up and be a responsible human being. And she's raised two daughters in her own image. If it weren't for Kat, you, and your mom, Luna never would have finished college. At least she did that and has a job teaching, but from what I can see, she's always a victim, just like her mother and sister. It's sad and a waste of life. I always wanted Missy to be more like you. She was such a troublemaker, and you were such a sweetheart."

"And therein lies the problem," I stated. "Telling her to be more like me was not conducive to her becoming her own person."

"Do you think if I were in their lives, they would be more responsible people?" Dad speculated.

"Probably not, but it would put to rest some of the dysfunctional nonsense," I replied.

"You're right, Addie, I haven't been the most responsible bird in the sky. Do you think Missy and her girls would do some family therapy?"

"They don't think anything is wrong with them," I responded. "They think the problems lie with us. But let's not give up. I'll feel Missy out on the subject when I see her and let you know what she says."

"That sounds like the beginning of a solid plan," Dad said. "Thank you, my beautiful princess. I see people waiting for me in the conference room, so I'd better get in there. I love you."

"I love you, too, Dad. Take care." I hung up and crossed my fingers that Missy would even speak to me.

Chapter 10: On My Way

Wednesday, October 9, 1996

I was tucked into a first-class seat on a flight headed for Atlanta. I decided to leave a day early so I could look up my ill-tempered little sister, Missy, who now lived and worked in Atlanta due to the demise of her last marriage—number six. I once told her she didn't have to marry every man she slept with. Her response was, "But that's the point."

I wanted to see if we couldn't restore a little order to our family. Neither Dale, Mom, nor I had spoken to Missy since her frivolous lawsuit failed about six months ago. Dale said he'd had enough drama in his life; he needed a break from Missy. Mom said she loved her last-born baby chick, but she hadn't had a headache since Missy tore up our check and stormed out of the courtroom yelling, "You can't buy me out of this family."

And, while I didn't appreciate the drama either, I didn't like our family being torn apart. I saw six months turning into two years very rapidly. Missy is a bra fitter for a department store in Atlanta. I thought I'd go to the department store and catch her on a break. I didn't think she'd yell and scream at me at the place of her employment. At least, I hoped not.

After getting comfy in my seat, ordering a glass of white wine, and choosing my dinner entrée, I began reading Elizabeth George's new book, *In the Presence of the Enemy*. I felt, more than saw, a man walking by from the restroom. I looked up. He wore worn jeans, a baggy sweatshirt, a Dodgers baseball cap, and dark glasses. I only had him in my sight for a couple of seconds, but he had a slouch akin to Lars's. I snickered to myself; Lars wouldn't be caught dead in that outfit.

After landing, I successfully collected my Beemer, which, as it turned out, was a convertible. I checked into my room at the Hotel Indigo, unpacked, and was soon sound asleep floating in the lap of luxury. My dream wasn't luxurious, however. I dreamed about Expert Doc, chewing on his cigar, with invoices raining over him. Lars laughed and picked up the invoices, stuffing them in his pockets. Then Expert Doc pulled hundred-dollar bills from his pockets and tossed them in the air. Lars was trying to catch them. Suddenly, they were on a boat in the middle of a lake. They had bright lights and appeared to be searching for something in the water. Their boat hit a rock, causing it to sink. They climbed up the rock and looked toward the shore. It wasn't far, but it was clear Expert Doc was scared. Lars stripped down to his briefs, jumped in the water, and began swimming toward shore.

At that moment, I woke up because I'd pushed off my covers and was freezing cold. I fell back asleep, but the dream didn't return. Thank goodness.

Chapter 11: The Crash
Thursday, October 10, 1996

I took my time reading the papers and enjoying my continental breakfast with plenty of coffee. I'd hoped to catch Missy near lunch time, so around 11:30 I called down for my car and headed for Whitman's Department Store in downtown Atlanta. I made my way to the lingerie department and found Missy chatting with a customer. "Mrs. Knockers, that is the proper bra fit."

"It feels so not-right. Are you sure?"

"I've fit hundreds of women in brassieres. Trust me, I know what I'm doing."

"If I can't get used to it, can I return it?"

"Of course; Whitman's is known for its return policy. Whitty wants happy, perky women."

"Okay. Ring me up. I'll be right out."

As Missy's customer sauntered out of the store, I made a beeline for her. "Hey, I'd like to talk to you when you have time to take a break."

"Good grief, Addie, you gave me the fright of my life. I didn't see you coming." She looked like a startled hornet.

"Sorry, I didn't mean to frighten you. You look terrific, by the way." Missy loves to be complimented on her beauty.

"Yeah, I got some nips and tucks a few months ago. Listen, Addie, I have nothing to say to you.

Mom always puts you and Dale ahead of me. I'm just an orphan. She should have put her property in my name, too."

"Mom says you sell or give away everything she gives you," I said. "She didn't want problems with the property, so she thought it was best to just give you your cash up-front. That way you wouldn't be tangled up in the property with Dale and me, and you could do what you pleased with the money."

"You and Dale always get everything," Missy whined. "I get nothing. That property will go up in value, and you want me to settle for what it's currently worth? That's not fair."

"No, it isn't," I agreed. "Apparently, you didn't read the documents we sent you. We agreed to give you your share of the inflated value as it increases. In effect, you'll receive a tidy little income every year."

"I'm forty-six years old. I don't need you guys doling out money to me," Missy snapped. "Besides, I want the property in my name only. Dale is super wealthy, and Mom and Dad gave you the Santa Monica house. You guys will always be okay. I have nothing."

"That's why Mom wrote it up this way. She wants to be sure you don't sell the property and that you have a steady income every year. She and Dad gave you half a million dollars on your fortieth birthday, and you have nothing left. It appears that you lived extravagantly, and now you're broke. We'd hoped you'd get your GED and a college education."

"Oh, for heaven's sake, you know how I feel about school," she barked. "The only thing it got me was pregnant. I don't need a high school diploma. Now get out of my face. I came in early so I could leave early. I have a golf game in an hour."

"How about I follow you out to the golf course, and—"

"No," she shouted.

"—And I'll buy martinis and dinner after your game," I continued.

"Martinis and dinner at Jameson's?" Missy asked, excitedly.

"Yep."

"That's the most expensive restaurant in the city," Missy tested.

"I'm good for it."

"Okay. If you have your Garmin with you, you can GPS it, but you can follow me, too. Meet me at the exit to the parking area."

***

I took the elevator down to the parking garage, retrieved my Beemer, and waited for Missy at the exit. I caught up to her and followed her out of the city and down the highway. We turned onto a two-lane road that was in dire need of paving. Missy sped up in her little Lexus sports coupe while I slowed down.

Suddenly, Missy's car spun out of control and disappeared down a hill. I hit the gas to catch up, slammed the brakes, and jumped out of my running car, sliding down the hill.

Missy's car had hit a tree.

"Missy, Missy!" I screamed.

From the driver's window, she was slumped over the wheel and bleeding from a wound on her head. I couldn't get the door open, but fortunately the window was rolled down, because the passenger side of the car looked like a broken accordion. I reached through the window and tried to get the seatbelt off her, but it was stuck. Running back to my car, I retrieved my Swiss Army knife from my purse. I hurried back to the car and began sawing at the seatbelt with the knife. It worked. It cut through the seatbelt, and I reached in, pulling Missy out of the car. I pulled and pulled, but could only get her halfway out. I pushed Missy back into her seat and leaned in through the window to see what was holding her back. Her shoe was caught under the brake. I wiggled her foot out of the shoe, grabbed her under the arms, and pulled hard. Suddenly free, Missy's body fell out the window, knocking me down, and landing on top of me. The wind was knocked out of me, but I pushed her off me, stumbled to my feet, and dragged her as far up the hill as I could.

There was a huge explosion as the car burst into flames. I threw myself on top of Missy. The heat from the flames was so intense, it felt like my skin had been seared. We had to get further away. I struggled to my feet and dragged Missy further away. The hill looked too ominous to attempt to get up, so I dragged Missy perpendicular to the hill, which enabled me to get more distance between us and the burning car. When I felt we were safely away from the fire, I bent down and felt for Missy' pulse. Thankfully, there was one—unless I was so nervous and full of adrenaline that I was imagining it.

I scurried up the hill to the Beemer, grabbed my mobile, flipped it open and called 911 as I slid back down the hill toward Missy. I didn't know the directions, but the operator told me not to worry, the police cars were equipped with Garmin GPS devices. I told her we'd be easy to spot because my rental car was in the middle of the road and a second car was on fire just down the hill. She remained on the line with me while the police, firemen, and paramedics were en route. I talked to Missy, telling her to wake up. I patted her cheeks a bit, but I was afraid to move her too much more. There was no telling what further damage I had done to her by dragging her across the dead foliage, dirt, and rocks.

It didn't take long for the emergency crew to reach us. They put Missy on a stretcher and got her up the hill to the ambulance where they gave her an IV and began assessing her injuries. My skin was bright red, and I was scratched and bleeding from head to foot, so the paramedics drove my car to the side of the road, locked it, and put me in the ambulance with Missy.

At the hospital, she was whisked in one direction, and I in another. The doctor didn't think I had any internal injuries, nor did I think I did, but I was so full of dirt and soot that he had me get in a shower to clean off with an antiseptic soap so my external injuries could be treated. My skin was hot and flushed from the intense heat, but I didn't have any serious burns. My hair was badly singed. Chris, who was my hairdresser as well as Jaime's partner, was going to go crazy when he saw it.

The doctor wanted me to stay overnight in the hospital for observation, but I insisted on going back to the luxury of my hotel room. Meanwhile, Missy had a broken hip, leg, and collarbone, as well as a concussion and a nasty cut across her forehead. She would be in surgery for the next five or six hours, so I borrowed some sweats from a nurse and took a cab back to the hotel, where I put on some clean clothes and ordered a martini sent up to my room ASAP.

Then I called the Smiley firm and left a message letting them know they'd have to get another reporter, at least for tomorrow, or reschedule tomorrow's depo. I was afraid that by tomorrow I might feel like a ping pong ball after a tournament. Next, I called the car rental company, told them what had happened, and asked if they would retrieve the Beemer and deliver it back to me at the hotel. My martini arrived. I took a few sips and began to relax. I didn't want to call Mom, Dad, or Dale and worry them about all of this because there was absolutely nothing they could do at the moment. So, I called Jaime. When I related what had happened; he went a little ballistic on me, but I managed to calm him down. I was okay, and Missy was going to live—albeit she'd have a long recovery period. Later, as I drifted off to sleep, I wondered what went wrong with Missy's car.

Chapter 12: Home
Friday, October 11, 1996

Bright and early, a secretary from the Smiley firm called to tell me they had no depos scheduled, and who the heck was I? I was stunned, but putting two and two together, I realized that someone had gone to a lot of trouble to have me implicated in two car accidents. I wonder if someone tampered with the brakes on Missy's car. I called Brent and asked him if he would follow up with the Atlanta Police Department to check out the brakes. My next call was to the hospital to check on Missy. Her doctor said the surgery went well. She'd been given a lot of pain meds, but she'd said she'd rather have a pitcher of martinis. I couldn't blame her there. Missy was going to need someone here to take care of her, so I called my eldest niece, Luna. She didn't pick up my call until I mentioned that her mother had been in a bad accident in Atlanta and was in the hospital.

"What the f'!" was her cheerful response. And this is the educated one of my two nieces. The younger one followed in her mother's footsteps, dropping out of high school and having a baby.

"I think you might want to talk to your sister and figure out how you're going to arrange for your mother's care. I'm sure she'll be booted out of the hospital soon and sent to a short-term rehab center, but she's going to have a long recovery. She has a concussion, a broken collar bone, broken leg, and fractured hip bone."

"Cripes!" exclaimed Luna.

"Yes." I gave her the name and number of the hospital and hung up. A hot shower would have been on the agenda, but I took a bath instead, swinging my legs over the side of the tub, trying to keep the bandages on my arms and legs from getting wet.

Back at the hospital, Missy was awake and using her best language. "You f'g bitch, you pushed me off the road. You wanted to kill me. You've always hated me. You—"

"Wait! Wait! Hasn't anyone told you what happened?" I asked.

"No, I've been in and out of consciousness. When I saw you, I woke up real fast. Don't you go pulling any plugs on me. I'm watching you. You look like shit. What the hell happened to you? Did your car go over the hill when you pushed me off? You've stooped to low things in your life, Adeline, but trying to kill me is way over the top. I'm ringing for a nurse. I need someone in here to protect me from you."

"I didn't push you off the road," I said. "I ran down the hill and pulled you out of your car, dragging you as far away from the wreckage as possible. Just before it blew up, I might add. You're lucky I was behind you. If I hadn't been, what would be left of your body would be a puzzle lying on a slab in the morgue. Someone messed with your car. I'm guessing it's your brakes, and it's likely the same person who killed Jonesy. We need to figure out who would want both you and Jonesy dead."

"I have no idea who that could be. Wait! What? Jonesy's dead? Oh my word! I can't stay awake any longer. The drugs..." Missy passed out. I knew she was faking, but there was no point in calling her on it.

Leaving the hospital, I pressed the button on my Nokia 232 mobile phone to see if I had any messages. Dale not only had stock in Nokia, but he was one of their attorneys, so for Hanukkah and Christmas gifts last year he'd given all of us these new portable telephones. They're amazing. The message was from my youngest niece, Sunbeam.

"What the f' happened to my mother?" Sometimes it's hard to tell my two nieces apart. The message from Sunbeam continued. "Luna called me and told me I had to catch the next plane out of LAX to Atlanta. I just credit-carded a flight. I arrive at six o'clock tonight and will go directly to the hospital. I have a key to Mom's condo, so I'll stay there. Call me."

I called her back but had to leave a message. "Thank you for getting here so quickly. I'll catch the next flight home. Call me back when you can."

I managed to get a flight leaving in three hours. Perfect. I checked out of the hotel and headed for the airport. It was a bit of a hassle traveling with my court reporting equipment. It all fits neatly into a rolling bag, but can't be checked with other luggage because knocking it around could damage my

DataWriter, so I carry it on board with me. The laptop bag pulls away from the Velcro, leaving a slightly smaller bag for the stewardess to store. Meanwhile, going through security is always a challenge. They check every little aspect of my DataWriter and cords and ask me tons of questions before I'm free to walk through.

My stomach grumbled, telling me it was lunchtime, so I grabbed a decent-looking salad and called Jaime to let him know I'd be home tonight. I'd left my car at the airport, so I didn't need a ride. Next, I called Dale to let him know about Missy, but I had to leave a message because he was in court. Then I called Mom.

"What?" she exclaimed, "A car accident? What happened? Is Missy okay?"

"Yes, Mom, Missy is okay, though a bit banged up. Sunbeam is flying into Atlanta tonight to be with her." I didn't want to go into all the broken body parts; hence, I just said, "Missy will have to spend some time recovering, so it will be nice to have Sunbeam there with her. I should be home around six o'clock tonight. I'll pop over when I arrive."

"You'll be hungry. I'll make one of my casseroles. See you then, sweetie."

Oh, boy! Mom's famous casseroles tend to go right to my hips.

***

After arriving home, and before going over to Mom's, I called Jaime to see if this was a good time to check in with him for a minute.

"Yes, of course, darlin'," he answered. "Chris just made a pitcher of martinis. Your timing, as always, is impeccable."

I skipped down the stairs, as I used to do as a kid, and rang the bell. I was greeted with a martini in a beautiful crystal glass. I've always been a fan of the Thin Man movies with Myrna Loy and William Powell. Her wardrobe in those films was stunning. Like my mom, I'm in love with the fashions of the thirties and forties: luxurious silk gowns with fur capes, stylish suits and dresses with matching hats, shoes, and purses. And, of course, the ever-elegant martini in one of those dazzling crystal glasses was over-the-top decadent.

"Wow! Thank you," I said to Jaime. "You know how I love Chris's martinis. This is exactly what I need after the last harrowing forty-eight hours."

"You poor darlin'. Do tell us all."

Chris came into the room and dropped his jaw, "Sweetie, what happened to your hair? It looks simply dreadful."

"I know. The flames and heat coming from the burning car singed my hair. I hope you won't have to give me one of those pixie cuts. Kat will have a good laugh if you do. She's never forgiven me for giving her a pixie cut when she was too little to know better."

"I'll give you some product to put on it," Chris said. "Meanwhile, plan on spending your lunch hour with me tomorrow. It's the only time I can fit you in. I normally wouldn't work on my lunch hour, but this truly is an emergency."

"Thank you, Chris. You are a lifesaver," I responded gratefully.

Jaime asked anxiously, "What happened? I know about the accident, and that you pulled Missy out of the car, and she's in the hospital with lots of broken bones. Why you even speak to the girl, I'll never know. But how did the accident happen?"

"I think someone messed with her brakes, just like Jonesy's," I answered. "And someone put me in both places at the time of the accidents—someone who doesn't know me very well, or they'd know about my high school job as an undercover officer for the Santa Monica Police Department. I'd never be suspected of murder. I called the Smiley firm to let them know I couldn't report the first day of depos only to find out there were no depos, and they'd never heard of me. The question is, who called and set up that too-good-to-be-true offer? And why?"

"I have the number they called from," Jaime reported. "I'll check it out first thing in the morning. We'll also have to find out who paid for this and how. There must be receipts. I'll follow up on that as well. Hey, have you eaten? We have one of your mother's famous casseroles in the oven. Chris is on a kick of making recipes from the fifties."

"Oh, my goodness! Mom invited me over for a casserole."

"Go get her and tell her to bring her casserole," Jaime responded cheerfully. "We'll have a potluck."

***

It was late when I crawled into bed with Law and Order cuddled up to me. I had nothing scheduled for the rest of the week. I could sleep in. What a marvelous feeling. Still, my thoughts tumbled around: who is trying to kill people, and why?

Chapter 13: The Chase

Saturday, October 12, 1996

I didn't wake up until ten o'clock. I never sleep that late. I wanted to go for a run down to Palisades Park, but with all my bandages and bruises, a slow walk was more in order. After my walk, I bought a latte from my favorite vendor, cleaned up, and made it to Chris's salon by noon. Chris's place was on San Vicente in a very posh part of town. It takes months to get an appointment with him, or anyone else in his salon for that matter. I'm so lucky to be a member of the family. With a wash, some product, a few snips of the scissors, and a blow-dry, I came out looking and feeling fantastic.

I headed back home to check in with Jaime and see what he'd discovered about the people who set up the depos. I pulled Mini into the garage next to Mom's Bentley, which reminded me that I should talk to her about selling her car. She had a terrible scare coming home from a manicure appointment last December and announced that she was giving up driving. As I opened the door to get out of Mini, I saw Mom running from her cottage with a frying pan in hand, screaming, "You little piece of shit. I'm going to beat the living daylights out of you!"

Jaime ran out of his door, heading down the street as fast as lightning. Thirty years ago, he won a medal at the Olympics in the track events. Now he chased a figure clad in jeans and a black t-shirt, who jumped into a utility van and took off. The van was going away from us and too far down the street to catch a license number. I rushed over to Mom, grabbing her and giving her a fierce hug. "Are you alright?"

"Yes," she replied.

"What happened?" I asked anxiously.

"I was out in the garden for most of the morning, working on the roses. I went in to use the bathroom and refresh my water bottle when I heard someone in my office. I grabbed a pan from the kitchen. I thought I'd sneak into the office and hit him over the head, but he must have heard me coming. He ran out the front door and down the street. That's when you pulled up and Jaime started chasing him."

"That's crazy!" I declared. "We've never had such issues in this neighborhood. Mom, you have to keep the doors locked. And where is that emergency necklace I gave you?"

"I'm not going to wear that thing. That's for old people. It's ugly and it ruins the appearance of my outfits, even my cute little gardening clothes."

"Oy vey! What are we going to do with you?" I exclaimed. "Let's go take a look at your office."

Jaime came bounding back out of breath. "I kept running after the van, but he pulled into traffic, and I lost him. I couldn't even get a number off the license plate."

In the office, we were confronted with a room in shambles.

"Good grief!" said Mother. "I guess he was looking for money or credit cards, neither of which I keep in the office. Thank goodness my purse is upstairs in my closet."

"I'll call Brent and report this," I said, "but it doesn't look like anything is missing, does it?"

"Not that I can tell right now," she replied.

"He wasn't carrying anything, and it looked like he was wearing latex gloves," Jaime added.

"Well," I said, "it's not exactly a crime scene. Let's get this cleaned up."

Jaime told me that the phone number he had for the law firm in Atlanta was a prepaid mobile phone and that the flight, hotel, and rental car had been paid for in cash. No one could identify the person or persons who paid for it all. Further, the reservation was for two nights, so whoever set this up knew I'd be leaving right after the accident.

I called Brent to tell him we'd had a second attempted break-in, to see what he'd found out about the brakes on Missy's car, and to let him know what Jaime had learned.

"The brakes were tampered with, no question about that. It sure looks like someone attempted to kill Missy and set you up as the killer, Addie, but who? And why?"

***

I met Mom in the garden for cocktails. We phoned the hospital to check on Missy. She was awake and talkative. It was going to be an awkward conversation between Mom and Missy, as they hadn't spoken in six months. I pretended that a rose caught my attention and walked toward it. I asked Missy not to mention her failed lawsuit nor the extent of her injuries because it would only upset Mom. Missy's curt response was, "I'll tell my mother whatever I damn well please. You need to mind your own business." I walked back to Mom and handed her the phone. I hate it when Missy tells me, "you need" to do such and such. It's like a slap in the face.

Jaime wandered over with a cocktail in hand. "I put Baxter's depo transcript and exhibits together to send to the court and filed our copies. I'm shocked at how large his bills are. The cost of medical attention is really out of hand. A nickel for a Q-tip, a dime for a paper cup. Can you believe that? He bills for a lot of time with his patients and runs numerous tests that don't appear to be necessary under the circumstances. Do you think he's padding his invoices and afraid of getting caught? Maybe Jonesy knew he was scamming, and the doc had to knock off Jonesy to save himself."

"Could be, but that doesn't explain Missy's accident. And if Lars killed Jonesy, that doesn't explain Missy's accident either. And someone wanted me implicated, someone who doesn't know my history. That could be either Lars or Expert Doc."

Chapter 14: Fog and Quilts

Sunday, October 13, 1996

I had a fitful night's sleep and woke to a cloudy, foggy Sunday morning. I'd dreamed about Gabe again. He was in a wheelchair, wheeling down a boardwalk, and I was running to catch up to him, but I wasn't fast enough. He disappeared into the fog.

My dream reminded me of the time Gabe had just finished an assignment in England and was taking a week off, so I flew over to spend the week with him. We stayed at the Savoy, the epitome of luxury. We went to Covent Garden and saw an opera at the Royal Opera House. We had martinis at the Dirty Martini Bar, and when we left the bar, the fog was so thick, I lost Gabe. I couldn't see him, and the music playing in the Garden was so loud, I couldn't hear him. I panicked. I was blind, deaf, and I was lost. But for my feet on the ground, I wouldn't have known which way was up. I stood still, trembling from the inside out, not knowing where to turn. Suddenly, Gabe's arms wrapped around me. I held him tight, so grateful that he'd found me. We made our way back to the hotel, snuggled up under the covers, and enjoyed the warm and exciting sensations of each other's bodies.

My mind returned to the present. My quilt group was meeting at my house today at eleven, so I had to get ready for them. I put the leaves in my dining room table, put the pads on top, set up another table, and brought out the Halloween quilt we were working on to be raffled off at the Halloween Festival downtown. I also made coffee and prepared a light lunch.

Mom came over with Halloween cookies. She set up her sewing machine, bright light, and magnifier. The gals arrived and the whir of sewing machines started up. There were only six of us today. Sally was on vacation, and Peony was working at the clinic. She's an ob-gyn and makes a quilt for almost every baby she delivers. We finished the Halloween quilt except for the binding, which I agreed to complete and deliver the quilt to the raffle booth.

The gals left around four o'clock. Mom and I cleaned up and put the house back to right. She declared she was too pooped to pop and just wanted to tuck in with her Janet Dawson mystery. I was feeling pretty much the same, so I walked her over to the cottage and returned home to settle in front of the fireplace with Susan Dunlap's new book, *Sudden Exposure*.

Chapter 15: Office Hanky-Panky
Monday, October 14, 1996

I called Valentin to see if he had time to do some investigating. Valentin served in 'Nam. He parachuted out of a plane and landed in a tree. After getting tangled in the chute, he tried to cut himself free, but fell out of the tree and severed his spine, putting him in a wheelchair.

That also ended his dream of becoming a cop, so he took an alternate route and became a PI. He looks like a fifty-year-old Jackie Cooper in *Peck's Bad Boy*. I filled him in on what was going on, gave him the cast of characters, and asked him to see what he could find out.

My injuries were rapidly improving, but to err on the side of caution, I decided to go for a slow run and walk out in Malibu Canyon. I hoped a change of scenery would help me shake out the mystery surrounding Jonesy's death and the attempt on Missy's life, but it just put me deeper into thought. Maybe the two things aren't connected. Baxter is the most likely suspect in Jonesy's death. He had motive, but what about means and opportunity? He was being held in security, but did Tommy have him in sight the entire time he was there? Maybe Tommy had to leave security for a few minutes. Maybe Baxter left momentarily to use the restroom. If you know what you're doing, it only takes a few minutes to mess with the brakes. I know that because when Dale was a teenager, he had a fascination for taking cars apart. A few of them got restored to working vehicles because I pitched in and helped when Mom wanted her garage back. I learned a few things.

Running in the canyon with the views of the ocean spreading before me is an ethereal experience. I'm lucky to live here and be surrounded by this beauty. I thank Dad every day for bringing us to this phenomenal place. I ran slow and easy. My muscles relaxed, and my mind drifted back to the case at hand. If Baxter was in trouble with the law or government and Jonesy knew that, we certainly have motive. If Tommy took his eyes off Baxter for a few minutes, we have opportunity. I'd have to assume that Baxter knew something about the mechanics of a car. That would explain Jonesy, but not Missy. Who would want Missy dead?

Oh goodness. I hate to admit it, but she's crossed lots of people. The question that should be asked is, who wouldn't want her dead? Missy's hateful and mean as hell. Someone could have heard about Jonesy's death and decided to do a copycat killing and throw Missy under the bridge. There's a little bit of money involved, but the only people to benefit from Missy's death are her daughters, and I can't see them killing their mother. They idolize her and are always fighting for her love and attention.

I adjusted my run to a slow walk as my mobile rang. It was Jaime.

"Addie, I've been looking at the exhibits in the Medi-Cal fraud case. Since there are several plaintiffs, there are a lot of bills entered into evidence. I mean, we know Expert Doc pads his bills, but if you do a cross-check, add up the padding of each patient's bills, and then add the padded residual from each bill, we're talking thousands of dollars, and we only have a few plaintiffs here. Imagine what the man is doing in the long-haul, with hundreds, maybe thousands of patients. If Jonesy figured this out, Expert Doc would have to get rid of him."

"Wow! Good work, Jaime. It doesn't figure in the attempt on Missy's life, but she has a lot of serious enemies. Maybe someone saw an opportunity and attempted a copycat killing to get rid of her."

"That girl should start making amends or hire a bodyguard," Jaime declared.

"From your mouth to God's ears," I responded. "Dale and I have tried talking to her, you know, but it's like talking to a wall. She won't listen. Mom and Dad's divorce really rocked Dale and me off our pedestals, but, with Missy's abandonment issues and low self- esteem, she never got past the devastation it wreaked on our family. She refused to do any therapy, and as a result, she gets angrier and meaner with each passing year."

"The padded bills in evidence might explain the attempted break-in at home, maybe even the one at your Mom's," Jaime continued. "Expert Doc may be worried that someone else could figure this out. He must be looking for something specific, but what?—The office phone is ringing. Talk to you later. Bye."

At home I showered and took some sandwiches over to Mom for lunch. The fog was rolling in, so we decided to eat in the kitchen rather than the garden. Mom had just put down her knitting, something a sight-impaired person can do if they're familiar with the craft. "What are you working on, Mom?"

"A little layette set for Nancy Newsome's baby. I should probably knit one for Norma as well. They've become good friends. They met at the Lamaze class. Now they ride together and wouldn't think of missing a session."

"That could explain why Norma left the office early the day Jonesy went over the canyon," I mused. "Although, she could have tampered with those brakes any time that afternoon."

"Oh, I can't imagine a friend of Nancy's committing murder," Mom retorted. "Nancy is such a good judge of character."

Jaime waved at me through the kitchen door, "Hey darlin', you want to pick up a quick afternoon depo and save Kelly's balls? To put it bluntly. His attorney has a depo, and Kelly forgot to schedule a reporter. His mind has been on that hot personal trainer that walked into his life a couple months ago. The guy is built like Adonis. Kelly's been deliberating on whether to ask him to move in. I told him it's way too soon. Anyway, about the depo, it's just over on Third Street."

"Sure, I'll do it. Tell Kelly I'll be there in half an hour."

***

I arrived in record time, but the depo wasn't scheduled to begin for another hour, so I took a walk down Third Street. Third Street was converted into an outdoor mall in 1963. When we were kids, it was a through street. I used to save my babysitting money and walk downtown to Henshey's Department Store to buy a new Nancy Drew book for myself and a Hardy Boys for Dale. What carefree days; reading books, meeting friends at the beach. Missy's six years younger than I am, and, as Dad and I discussed, our parents were always telling her to be more like me. Parenting was different in the fifties than it is in the nineties. Still, I'd cringe when I'd hear them say, "Why can't you be more like your sister? She's so good," implying that Missy was bad—but she wasn't; she was just active. I'm sure they told her that because they were so frustrated. I read and played quietly. Dale played in the yard with his friends, making up games or playing baseball. Missy ran around the neighborhood tormenting anyone that crossed her path. When kids saw her coming, they ran into their houses crying, "Help! Mom! Missy's outside!"

I was always Dad's princess and Dale was his pal. Poor Missy was the Holy Terror. My dad hadn't really wanted any more children, but he was excited when Mom was pregnant and he thought Missy might be another boy. When it turned out he had another daughter, he was disappointed, and Missy felt that disappointment. As a child, Missy sought attention by having temper tantrums and lying, but she didn't get the sort of attention she was seeking. Missy was a beautiful child, and she's a knockdown gorgeous woman today. I wish she would get some help and find some happiness. She has on occasion attempted suicide to garner attention. When I found out what she was doing, I made an appointment for her to see a psychologist. I paid for it, and Dale and I dragged her into the car and drove her to the appointment, where we walked her in and waited for her. When the session ended and she joined us in the waiting room, she said, "That f'ing bitch made me cry. I'm never coming back."

It was farmers' market day on Third Street, and I went a bit crazy buying all sorts of fruits, veggies, and sundry items. I bought so much that I had to take them to my car before heading back to the law firm. Now I was running a bit late, so I was glad I was all set up and ready to go.

The depo was of a woman who witnessed an accident involving none other than Expert Doc. It appears that the doc not only padded his bills, but he had a drinking problem to boot. Counsel taking the depo was the same opposing counsel in the Medi-Cal fraud case, Mr. Appel, and, of course, Lars was Expert Doc's attorney. Expert Doc, who looked like he'd been on a bender the night before, sat in on the depo, chewing away on his cigar.

I swore in the witness, a sweet-looking, elderly lady dressed in a belted black dress and sensible black shoes. Counsel began the preliminary questioning, but his eyes were on Expert Doc, who sat across from him, next to Lars. I glanced at Expert Doc. He was sweating profusely, his eyes looked glassy, and the cigar dangled off his lips. Counsel had just gotten into the meat of the questioning when we heard a thump and glanced over to see Expert Doc had fallen forward, hitting his head on the table, his cigar stuck in his mouth. I quickly typed in, "Expert Doc passes out, 2:53 p.m. Off the record."

"Oh dear!" the witness exclaimed.

Expert Doc had been drinking a chocolate mint milkshake, which he knocked into Lars's lap as he passed out. Lars jumped up with green chocolate ice cream running down his shirt and pants. He was trying to wipe it off, but that only made it worse. He stormed out of the conference room heading toward the men's room. Counsel Appel and I tried rousing Expert Doc, but he was really out of it.

"He doesn't appear to be drunk," I said, feeling for a pulse. I couldn't find one. "Appel, see if you can get a pulse. I'm calling 911."

Kelly heard the commotion and came out of his office. "What's going on?" he asked.

"Expert Doc passed out," I answered. "We're having trouble getting a pulse. I just called 911."

Kelly and I hurried into the conference room where Appel was doing CPR on Expert Doc.

"The paramedics are on their way. Did you get a pulse?" I asked.

"I think so. It's very weak."

"What happened to Lars and our witness?" I asked Appel.

"The witness went to the ladies' room, and I assume Lars is still in the men's room trying to clean chocolate mint ice cream off his Armani suit."

Sirens drew close, and a minute later, two paramedics rushed in and took over for Appel. Another paramedic asked us to follow her into the reception area. Appel excused himself and headed toward the men's room. When Kelly said he hadn't been in the conference room and only just came on the scene, the paramedic focused on me, asking for my name, address, phone number, and what I was doing here today. When I told her I was reporting the depo, she said, "So, you were right there. What happened?"

"When I came into the room, Expert Doc was seated next to Attorney Larceny. The doc didn't look too good. He has a drinking problem, so I thought perhaps he'd been on a bender the night before. He was sweating profusely, and his eyes were glazed over. We weren't too far into the depo when all of a sudden, he fell forward, hitting his head on the table, and the milkshake he'd been drinking landed in Larceny's lap. Larceny a mess and went directly into the men's room to clean up. The witness went to the ladies' room. When

Appel and I couldn't wake the doc, I tried getting a pulse. I couldn't get one, so I asked Appel to take over while I ran into the reception area to phone 911."

"Do you know where the doc got the milkshake?"

Kelly joined in, "Yes, I got it for him from the ice cream shop across the street." Appel came out of the men's room and joined us.

"Did you leave the milk shake unattended at any time?" the paramedic asked Kelly.

"No."

"Who else was present when you gave the drink to the doc?"

"Just Larceny and the witness. Appel was in his office. Addie hadn't arrived yet."

Just then, one of the paramedics working on Expert Doc came out and said, "The doc has a pulse, but it's very weak. We're transferring him to Santa Monica Hospital stat."

They rushed out the door with the doc on a stretcher. The other paramedic quickly bagged the milkshake container and left with them. Kelly and Appel and I just looked at each other.

"What the heck just happened?" Kelly said. "That was crazy!"

"I know. Right? It just all happened so fast. I can't believe it. Since they bagged the milkshake, it looks like they suspect poisoning," I answered.

"Yikes!" Kelly spoke up.

Appel piped in, "There's a bottle of Macallan in the kitchen. Would you guys like a shot? I could definitely use one."

"Yes!" we said in unison and followed Appel into the kitchen, where he poured three shot glasses and handed us each one. We clinked glasses. Kelly downed his. I took a sip. Then I suddenly remembered our witness.

"Oh, my gosh! What happened to our witness?"

We checked the restroom, but she wasn't there. We went into the conference room, and there she was.

"Are we continuing?" she asked.

"Not today," Appel said. "The doc was taken to the hospital."

"Oh dear! That must have happened while I was in the ladies' room. Well, then I'll be off."

"Did you happen to see where Mr. Larceny went?" I asked.

"I saw him go outside just before I went to the restroom. He was dripping chocolate mint ice cream all over. I didn't see him again after I returned."

I checked outside, but Lars was nowhere around. "He's such a scumbag," Kelly declared.

"You won't get an argument from me on that one," I replied.

I packed up my equipment and checked my messages. I had a message from Valentin saying to give him a call. I decided to wait until I got home to call him in the privacy of my office. Traffic in downtown Santa Monica was so bad, it took me half an hour to drive a fifteen-minute walk. I climbed the stairs to my flat and instantly kicked off my stilettos, walked to my closet, and slipped into my UGGs. When Mom and Dad gave me this house, Mom had converted what was a nursery off the master bedroom into a gorgeous walk-in closet, which now housed my rather extensive wardrobe. My favorite piece of clothing is the dark green, cable-knit, boatneck-collar sweater Mom knit for me when I was in high school. The sleeves turned out to be way too long, but I just roll them up. Mom so appreciates that I still have that sweater, love it, and wear it.

I took my equipment into my office and returned Valentin's call. "Addie, I'm glad you got back to me so quickly. I turned up some interesting information. Expert Doc and Larceny were in the same fraternity at Harvard. One of their fraternity brothers went missing, Hank Gould. His body and sports car turned up ten years later when Lost Lake was drained. Guess what?"

"What?" I asked anxiously.

"The brakes on the sports car were tampered with."

"Holy Toledo!" I exclaimed.

"Yep. And there's more," Valentin continued. "It turns out that Expert Doc and Larceny had part-time jobs at an auto mechanic's shop."

"Oy vey!" I said, surprised.

"Yeah," Valentin went on, "I've got a call in to the local PD back there to see what else I can find out. I was able to track down the owner of the mechanic shop at that time. He said he remembered

Expert Doc and Larceny well. They were smart, quick learners, and didn't mind getting their hands dirty, unlike some other students he had working for him."

"Great Scott! There's means and opportunity, but what could possibly be the motive? We need to turn this over to Brent," I decided.

"Absolutely!" Valentin confirmed. "I'll give him a call, and I'll let you know what I learn from the PD."

"And guess what else? Expert Doc passed out during a deposition today," I added. "We thought he was drunk, but it looks like it may be more serious. He's in the hospital now."

"Wow! He might have some underlying health issues," Valentin offered.

"Or he was poisoned," I speculated.

I'd no sooner disconnected from Valentin than Chris called. "We have a pitcher of Colonel Nimetz's Manhattans. I'll collect your mom and meet you in the garden in ten."

"Sounds deadly! I'll be right down."

We all love the garden and spend as much time there as we can. Grandma Henkey had been passionate about her garden, and my father followed in her footsteps. Mom's grandma loved gardening as well, and Mom spent many school holidays under her tutelage. Together my parents created this sanctuary full of fruit trees, roses, shrubs, foxglove, flowering quince, heather, and magnolias. There are benches and chairs strategically situated for privacy and intimate talks. Their garden was on the Santa Monica Garden Tour for many years.

I slipped into a comfy pair of jeans and tennies, grabbed a sweater, and headed down to the garden. Mom, Chris, and Jaime were chatting away and sipping their drinks. In the spirit of the upcoming holiday, Jaime had selected cocktail picks with witches' hats on them. I sat down and joined them, savoring the luscious garden smells wafting in the ocean air. I was just filling them in on Valentin's discoveries when my mobile began playing "Raindrops Keep Falling on My Head," my ringtone for Luna because that was her favorite song when she was a little girl.

"Aunt Addie! You...won't believe—" I could tell that she was upset. She was stumbling on her words.

"Luna, darling, take some deep breaths. Do you mind if I put you on the speakerphone? I'm in the garden with Jaime, Chris, and Grandma."

"No, that's fine," Luna said. "Mom drank a ton of martinis this afternoon. And she's also on painkillers. This is not a good combination. She's okay; however, in her drunken, drugged state, she told me the wildest story. You're not even going to believe this: she's been sleeping with Lars. Before her accident, Lars would occasionally fly her out to Los Angeles for a weekend of sex. That just grosses me out. She began babbling on about it because she's scared to death. Apparently, he liked her to come to his office wearing a trench coat with varying displays of nearly no clothing underneath. I mean, you should see her lingerie wardrobe. It's way over the top. We're talking Adam and Eve, Ann Summers, Frederick's—"

"Okay. We get the idea," I told her.

"Yeah. We're not exactly the Partridge girls," Luna said. "Anyway, apparently, she and Lars were going at it on his desk in his office when he gets a call he just has to take and barges out of the room. There she is, left lying on the desk, panting, as she puts it. It's so gross. She's nearly naked and sweaty. Papers are sticking to her skin. As she begins pulling them off, she notices a note, 'I can't be a party to your murdering and scamming Medi-Cal any longer. I'm not going to spend the rest of my life in prison covering up for you and…,' before she could finish reading, Lars came rushing back into the room.

"She quickly tucked the note in between some other documents, but she's pretty sure Lars knew she saw it. So, now she's afraid that if Jonesy saw that note, Lars may have killed him, and if Lars thinks she read the note, he might be trying to get rid of her, too. You have to admit, two incidents of tampered brakes are very fishy."

Jaime interjected, "I can't believe that girl would stoop to sleeping with Lars. It actually grosses me out, too."

Luna added, "Well, you know, she owed him a lot of money from that stupid lawsuit she filed against Aunt Addie and Uncle Dale. I think she's working off her debt; you know what I mean?"

"Yes, we do," I replied. "But don't worry. Your mom has a top-of-the-line security system in her condo. However, I'll relay this info to Brent."

"I hope he doesn't get grossed out," Luna said with concern. "They dated in high school, you know."

"I can't forget it," I admitted. "She dumped him, and he's never gotten over it. How is your mom, other than overdoing martinis and pain pills?"

"She's really hurting and needs a lot of help," Luna answered. "She's well-insured from her last marriage, which is good, because her home care is covered, so we have two nurses taking twelve-hour shifts. Thank goodness! Because I'm a teacher, not a nurse."

"Gotcha," I said.

"I'll let you guys go," replied Luna.

"Okay. And I'll pass on this information to Brent," I added.

"Oh, thank you. I feel so much better. Bye Grandma, Jaime, Chris."

"Well," I said, "that might explain Jonesy's murder and the attempt on Missy's life. Jonesy may have uncovered some evidence exposing Lars's fraudulent activities, and Lars probably believes Missy saw something she shouldn't have."

I called Brent and left a message. Then we all walked down to the Broken Drum for dinner. I love reporting, but this time off is a real luxury. I wonder if I could afford to retire any time soon.

***

I'd just gotten into cozy pajamas and slipped into my UGG slippers when "Surfin' U.S.A.," my ring tone for Dale, started blaring from my mobile. "Hello, Little Brother." Dale is six-foot-two. I'm five-foot-two.

"Hey, Big Sis. What's happening? I got your message about Missy. Is she all right?"

"She's okay," I told him. "She'll have a long recovery. She has a concussion, a broken collarbone, broken leg, and fractured hip bone. She's lucky to be alive."

"Wow! What exactly happened?" Dale asked. "Did she overdo the martinis and get behind the wheel?"

"No, actually, someone messed with the brakes on her car." I proceeded to fill him in on the details, ending with, "So now we're trying to figure out who would want both Missy and Jonesy dead, and Lars is looking like the likely suspect."

"Listen, Ads," Dale admonished, "you could be in a bunch of danger. If you wouldn't mind, I'd like to put some extra security around you and Missy. She's a real pain in the arse, but I wouldn't want to see her killed. I'm betting Valentin will find a connection before the PD does."

"Actually, Valentin has found a connection," I said. "The three of them went to Harvard together, and Lars and Expert Doc worked in an auto mechanic's shop. Valentin relayed the information to Brent and said he'd call me when he learned more."

"Now we're getting somewhere," Dale piped in.

"Extra security is a good idea," I confirmed, "but I don't want you to flip for all the expense. I'll pay for our extra security here. You take care of Missy and the girls."

"I'll get the security," Dale insisted. "You put your money in the bank and get a stamp in your little black book." We both laughed, remembering that as kids, Grandma Hammersley, Mom's mom, had given us savings accounts. We had a contest going to see who could get the most stamps in their little black book.

After reminiscing about that for a moment, Dale said, "Ads, you know that I've been very fortunate financially, and nothing makes me happier than to be able to share that good fortune with my family and friends. I'll make arrangements with my security people and give Missy and Valentin a call."

"Okay," I said.

"I'd say, unfortunately I'm going to be here another week, but I'm having a great time working this case with Uncle Bud, so it's actually quite fortunate," Dale told me.

"Oh, I know!" I acknowledged. "I had so much fun reporting that ice cream case for him. He's astounding in the courtroom. And we'd get up early in the morning and go running before going to work. I think it's time I made another trip back to Wisconsin. Mom would love to go, too."

"Speaking of Mother, I'll check in with her as well. How's she doing?"

"She's feisty as ever. She went after the intruder with a frying pan," I laughed.

"Isn't that just like her?" Dale laughed, too. "Have you talked to Dad? We should let him know what's going on."

"I spoke to him just before I went to Atlanta. I'll give him another call."

"I don't think that was a random attempted theft. Somebody is looking for something you have," Dale stated.

"I agree. And we have to figure out what it is."

"Meanwhile, watch your back, Ads. I think you should call Brent and ask him to have a squad car circle the neighborhood periodically."

"I hate to bother him with that, but okay."

"I scheduled a return flight for Wednesday, the twenty-third," he said.

"I'll pick you up."

"That would be great," Dale exclaimed. "We can catch up on the drive back to the beach. And don't forget, we have the Halloween party on the twenty-sixth."

"I could never forget that," I said.

"I'd better go. Best wishes to Jaime and Chris. We'll talk soon. Love you, Ads!"

"Love you, too, Little Brother!"

Chapter 16: Doc's Accident
Tuesday, October 15, 1996

Law and Order woke me up at 5:30 in the morning. Law batted his ball around the bed, and Order chased a ribbon. I've tried closing them out of the room, but it takes all of ten seconds for them to hit the door handle and march back in. Cats! You gotta love 'em, right?

I tossed on my running shirt, shorts, and shoes, and headed out the door for Palisades Park. It was a cool, brisk morning, perfect for a run. I ran through Palisades Park to downtown, where the smell of baking bread enveloped me. I stopped and bought four loaves of fresh sourdough: one for Mom, Jaime, Chris, and myself. Back home, I showered and made some eggs to go with my bread. The monsters, Law and Order, had, of course, gone back to bed. My mobile started blaring, "Hello, Dolly," my ring tone for Jaime. It's his favorite musical. "Good morning, Jaime! What's up?"

"First, I just spoke to Kelly. Expert Doc was poisoned, but he's going to be okay. He'll probably be released from the hospital today."

"Poisoned? Wow! If the paramedics hadn't bagged the milkshake, I never would have suspected. I wonder how it happened."

"Judging from who was present, my bet's on Lars. It's a good thing you were there and called 911 so promptly. You probably saved Expert Doc's life.

"The other thing I was calling about is that Kelly has another last-minute depo he needs to cover because, again, he forgot to schedule a reporter. I tell you he's got to get his mind off Mr. Hottie. Maybe they should move in together. You know how it is. Once you start living together, you're just like an old married couple. At any rate, do you want to take it? It's at ten o'clock."

"Oh, sure. Why not? Email the info to me."

***

I arrived at the law firm at 9:20 and set up my equipment. Turns out it was the depo of the police officer who was the first responder on the scene at drunken Expert Doc's auto accident. Appel was taking the depo. I swore in the witness, and Counsel began questioning. There's always a bunch of preliminaries before the real questioning begins, so it got interesting when he asked, "What happened when you arrived at the scene of the accident?"

"The doc's vehicle, a black Mercedes, had gone right through the plate glass window of Sur la Table at 301 Wilshire Boulevard. Doc was alone, sitting in his car. I asked him if he was injured. He said, 'No. What happened? Why are you here?' I said, 'Sir—' He corrected me, 'It's Doctor.' He reeked of alcohol. I suggested he step out of the car and have a seat on a nearby bench.

"He stumbled out of the vehicle, and I assisted him to the bench. I administered a breathalyzer test. The doc's alcohol level was .200. He couldn't walk a straight line. He was confused and yelling how he was on his way to 'kill some f'g son of a bitch.' At that point, the paramedics arrived and took over. We found his wallet on the front seat of the car and his registration in the glove box. Security arrived, along with the manager of the store, and bedlam broke out," the police officer answered.

There were some more follow-up questions, and then Counsel said, "Thank you, Officer. Let's take a short break so I can look at my notes, but I think we're about done."

I wandered down the hall to see if Kelly was in his office. I found him working at his computer. "Hi, Kelly! Jaime told me that Expert Doc was poisoned, but he'll be okay."

"Yes. Thank the universe!" Kelly responded.

"Who do you think could have poisoned him?" I asked.

"If I were a betting man, I'd say Lars."

"Jaime said the same thing," I commented. "I overheard a conversation where Lars and the doc were talking, and the doc said he didn't want to be involved anymore, he wanted out. They lowered their voices, so I didn't get to hear what it was all about, but if they're doing something illegal and Expert Doc wants out, maybe Lars did dump some poison in the milkshake."

"But when?" Kelly asked. "They were together the whole time. Surely Expert Doc would have noticed if Lars put something in his drink."

"It only takes a second to drop something in a drink," I said. "Lars could easily have distracted the doc. The toxicology report will answer some questions. Brent gets a copy of it. I'll check with him. How are you doing otherwise?"

Kelly replied, "Oh, you know, I'm good. It's been a ghastly week, though, I'll tell you."

"I hear you have a hot new boyfriend who's a personal trainer. Maybe I should check him out."

"I got to him first, Addie. Hands off. How are you doing with the online dating sites?"

"Well, I haven't exactly gotten to that project yet."

"What? You promised me a month ago you were going to diligently begin the search."

"I know, but I'm always so busy. I haven't found the time yet. And Gabe is only missing. We don't know that he's dead."

"Oh, honey, it's been four years. Gabe isn't coming back. You need to come to terms with this."

"You're right. I just miss him so much, Kelly. I can't believe he's gone. And Dale losing Annie to cancer just months after Gabe disappeared, sent us both into a tailspin that we're only just beginning to come out of. I think he and I have come to realize that these losses are not something a person gets over, but, rather, you learn to live with the pain and emptiness. We both need to move on. I want so much for Dale to find someone to complete and complement his life. He's so loving and deserving. I thought if I set an example by dating, maybe he would follow. Anyway, I see Counsel is ready to reconvene. You must bring Hottie over for cocktails one night. I'm dying to meet him."

After going back on the record, Counsel announced he had no further questions, and we adjourned for the day.

***

We had a transcript that needed to be delivered to a firm in the same building as Lars, so after the depo, I drove over there. Delivering transcripts is usually Jaime's job, but I told him I'd take this one because I wanted to have a chat with Tommy, the Head of Security in that building. All the evidence of murder and mayhem pointed directly at Lars, but I couldn't get our witness Baxter off my mind. We knew so little about him. I parked in a temporary parking slot and walked into the security office.

"Hi, Tommy, how's tricks? Have you had any more crazies leaping across tables?"

"Very funny, Addie. You have a habit of being around when crazy things happen. Remember the time that eight-foot tree got entered into evidence in the infamous tree case? We couldn't get it up in the elevator, so everyone had to traipse down here. You set up your equipment and took the testimony in the parking lobby. Then, because it was marked into evidence, you had to take custody of the tree, so I got my brother's truck and hauled it over to your place. What a day."

"It sure was." I exclaimed. "The attorneys ended up stipulating they were done with the tree, and they didn't care what I did with it. So, we planted it in our yard, and it's doing quite well."

"I told my daughter what an exciting job you have, and now she's checking in to going to court reporting college after she finishes with her BA," Tommy said.

"That's terrific! Let me know if she'd like to sit in with me on a few depos to test the waters.

"When you had Baxter down here, did you leave him alone for any amount of time? Maybe he asked to use the restroom? If he did, was he gone long enough to mess with Jonesy's car? If you know what you're doing, it only takes a few minutes."

"He was here for an hour and a half. I didn't have the manpower to babysit him. I had an emergency call on the twenty-sixth floor. I was gone for about twenty minutes. Then he asked to use the restroom. That took maybe fifteen minutes. But we've got security cameras all over the place. He'd be crazy to try anything. Well, he was acting crazy, wasn't he? You know what, I'll get the security tapes from that day, and we'll take a look."

"That's super, Tommy. Thank you. If it needs to be done officially, we can get Brent to okay it."

"Naw, I can handle it. I'll let you know what I find out."

"That's great. Is it okay to leave my car here while I deliver this transcript to the eighth floor?"

"It's fine."

"Back in a flash."

***

When I returned to the parking lot, Tommy was out of his office, so I got in Mini and headed out. I had to stop at the pet store to buy food for Law and Order; otherwise, they'd give me what-have-you when I got home. Then I went to the market and loaded up on supplies for Mom and myself. My last stop was the cleaners, where I ran into Norma picking up a bunch of dry cleaning that was not maternity clothes. In fact, one of the dresses looked very much like the dress Mrs. L. wore to Friday night services last week.

"Hey, Addie! You use Smith's Cleaners too, huh?"

"Yeah, Dad and Ron Smith go way back. Ron opened Smith's the same year Dad opened his helicopter school. In those days Dad brought all his uniforms in here. That's a load of dry cleaning you've got there."

"A secretary's duties often get pushed out of the office," Norma replied. "I'm running errands for Lars."

But I didn't see any of Lars's baggy suits in with the dresses.

I got home, put the food away, fed the monsters, sent my transcript to Patrice, and headed over to Mom's with her groceries. Jaime and Chris had tickets to see a play at the Geffen and left early to have dinner in Westwood. Mom was completely engaged in Janet Evanovich's *Two for the Dough*—large print, of course.

"Sorry, honey, I just can't put this book down. It's not only a well-written mystery, but it's funny as all get out. Can we talk later?" she apologized.

"Sure, Mom." I went back home and plopped down at my computer to see what online dating was all about.

Two and a half hours later, I was completely exhausted and had a date to meet a gentleman at the wine bar on Ocean Avenue the next night at five o'clock. His picture was pleasant. He was fifty-four years old—two years older than I—an entrepreneur, and he lived at the Marina. Maybe this online dating wouldn't be so bad after all.

Chapter 17: Follow the Money
Wednesday, October 16, 1996

The theme song from *Columbo* was wafting through my mobile on my bedside table. "Good morning, Valentin. You do realize it's seven o'clock in the morning and this is my week to sleep in since my too-good-to-be-true job really was too good to be true?"

"Oh, Law and Order would have had you awake in the next few minutes anyway. And I have some new findings to report. First, though, you'll see more people in the neighborhood than usual: a woman pushing a baby carriage, some ladies walking their dogs, joggers, race walkers of various sizes, that type of thing. That's the security Dale hired. Be sure to pass that info on to Vesta, Jaime, and Chris.

"Next, my further research revealed that Hank Gould, the body in the car in the lake, was engaged to be married to Mrs. L. I've already called Brent. We make it awfully easy for the SMPD, don't we?"

"Wow! That is some news," I responded. "It sounds like Lars, or maybe Expert Doc, offed Hank, but why? They had means and opportunity, but what's the motive?"

"Follow the money," advised Valentin. "Mrs. L. is the daughter of Joseph Goldman, owner of Farmington Enterprises. Back then, she was worth a lot of money—not so much now. Old Joseph made some bad investments, and Lars has squandered a great deal of Mrs. L.'s funds."

"Interesting. So, with Hank out of the way, Lars was able to swoop in and charm Mrs. L., marry her, and open his own law firm with access to all that money."

"There's more," Valentin offered. "Are you ready for this?"

"Ready? My earrings are twitching in anticipation."

"Norma Costello was Norma Gould before she married, and Hank Gould was her brother."

"You did dig up some history," I exclaimed. "But I can't see Norma or Mrs. L.—wait a minute. I ran into Norma at Smith's Dry Cleaners. She said she was picking up dry cleaning for Lars, but it was all women's clothing, and I recognized one of Mrs. L.'s dresses. Still, it wouldn't be unusual that they'd remain friends, and they had no motive for killing Jonesy or nearly killing Missy."

"Yeah, that's a stumper," he added.

"It sure is. Let me know if you come up with anything else."

"Okay. See ya, Boss."

"See ya, Valentin."

I attempted to go back to sleep, but as predicted, Law and Order had other ideas. I got up, saw to their needs, went for a brisk run, checked on Mom, and spent the rest of the day proofing. For a reporter, proofing is endless. Some reporters hire proofers as well as scopists, but I like to have the final eye on my product to make sure there are no faux pas.

Suddenly, it was four o'clock, and I needed to get ready for my online date at the wine bar. What to wear! I went for slacks, stilettos, and a cashmere sweater. I thought about walking, but twelve blocks in stilettos? Uh-uh. Not happening. So, I pulled Mini out of her garage and headed down to Ocean Avenue. I easily found parking on the street. The parking gods were with me tonight.

In the bar, I couldn't spot my date. Maybe he was just running late. Then I saw a gentleman, who looked to be in his late seventies, or early eighties, waving at me. I was trying to place the face. Was that someone I knew? He waved me over, so I walked toward him.

"Addie," he greeted me. "I'm Stan the Man from the online dating site."

My mouth fell open. "You lied about your age?"

"Only by a few years," he quibbled.

"Why would you do that? Whoever you meet is obviously going to know you lied."

"Nobody wants to go out with an old codger," he answered. "If I dissemble about my age, women will at least meet me, and I have a chance."

"But if you're honest, you'll likely meet a nice lady your own age," I theorized.

"Oh, women my age are old."

"I'd say it depends on your state of mind," I retorted. "At any rate, you'd be better suited for my mother, who, by the way, is single."

"If she looks like you, honey, I'm in," he said, raising his eyebrows. "As long as you're here, let me buy you a glass of wine."

As it turned out, he was eighty-two—eight years older than my dad, and ten years older than my mom. He was heavy into real estate investing, which is also an interest of mine. He was friendly and talkative and gave me a lot of good advice. All in all, it wasn't a bad evening.

Chapter 18: Blackmailing
Thursday, October 17, 1996

I woke up to "Raindrops Keep Fallin' on My Head."

"Luna, it's seven o'clock in the morning. I'm off work today. I want to sleep."

"I'm sorry, Aunt Addie. I know there's a time difference, but I was just so anxious to talk to you."

"And I'm sorry I snapped at you," I said. "Valentin called me at seven o'clock yesterday morning. Tonight, I'll turn my ringer off before I go to bed. At any rate, what's up?"

"Well, I was paying bills for Mom, and I noticed several unexplained deposits for five thousand dollars each. I asked Mom about them, and she said she couldn't remember. Now, maybe she can't. Her memory has been going in and out...but I'm not sure it isn't selective. Do you know anything about these deposits?"

"No, I don't," I answered.

"There were three of them; two weeks, four weeks, and six weeks before her accident."

"Fifteen thousand dollars!" I exclaimed. "I wonder what she's been up to."

"Yeah, with Mom you never know. Hopefully, her memory clears up soon."

"How's she doing otherwise?"

"She's a pain. Sunbeam is coming to relieve me next week. I'll be glad to get back to my classroom. Even kindergarteners aren't this demanding."

"Well, take care, sweetie, and keep me posted."

"I will. Bye, Aunt Addie."

I checked on Law and Order's food dishes and litter box, thinking with that handled I could go back to bed. I grabbed Marcia Muller's latest book, *The Broken Promise Land*, and crawled under the covers. It was a perfect Santa Monica morning for lounging in bed: misty and overcast.

I drifted off, and the next thing I knew, it was ten o'clock in the morning. I made myself an espresso and called Mom. I thought I'd skip my morning run and take her shopping and out to lunch. We love the Woodland Hills Mall, and I'm very much a believer in retail therapy. Shopping lifts my spirits. I adore the scents of all the products coming together in the cosmetic department, the fresh smell of new clothes, and the earthy fragrance of handbags in the boutiques, but my favorite is the essence of paper and ink in the bookstores. When I go shopping with Kat, she asks me to please turn my head when we walk past a bookstore. She has spent many an hour with me in bookstores while I read the dustjackets of the latest in mysteries.

Mom thought shopping was a terrific idea, so forty-five minutes later we were tucked into Mini and sitting on the 405 headed for the mall. Once again, the traffic gods were with us; we arrived in record time. We pay a monthly service for valet parking that includes a car wash. I love it. We decided to do a little shopping before eating lunch.

Mom had determined that the decade of her seventies was going to be about exercise. As well as playing a little tennis now and then, she'd faithfully been going to a senior exercise class at the parks and rec three days a week and now wanted to take up walking as well, so she needed some sturdy walking shoes. I took her to my favorite running shoe store and while she was trying on shoes, I walked out of the store to take a phone call.

It was the vet telling me it was time for Law and Order's next well-cat-care appointment. As I hung up, I saw Mrs. L. entering the baby furniture department at Macy's across the way. Why is Mrs. L. looking at baby furniture? Could she be pregnant? It's unlikely. She's in her fifties.

I pulled my scarf up over my head and wandered around as though browsing. Mrs. L. was at the sales counter talking to the clerk. She was just completing her purchase of—baby furniture? She was asking to have it delivered to 1684 Beverly Glen on the fifteenth of next month. That's her address!

Mom's voice startled me. "Addie, there you are. I've been looking all over for you. I got the perfect pair of walking shoes. What a lovely gentleman the salesclerk is. Let's go to lunch. I'm starving."

My cover was blown. I turned around and said, "Hi, Mrs. L. I didn't see you there. How are you?"

Mom piped right in, "How could you miss her? She's standing right next to you. And why do you have a scarf on your head? You look like you're hiding from someone."

I gave her "the look." That's Law's slit-eyed look, the one he gives me when he's trying to threaten me into giving him treats. I grabbed Mom's arm and turned her around, heading out the door. Over my shoulder, I said, "So nice bumping into you, Mrs. L. Have a lovely afternoon."

We had light salads and sparkling water at Nordstrom's café, did a little more shopping, and arrived home about five o'clock. Mom decided she'd like to take a short nap before dinner, so I plopped down in the garden, propped my feet up, and listened to messages on my mobile. Dale left a message that he was just checking up on us. Luna asked me to call her as soon as I could. Apparently, Missy poured out some more information after washing down a few pain pills with martinis. And Jaime asked me to call when I got home because, he said, "We're getting a lot of depositions scheduled in the next couple months. We might need help."

I called Dale back, but he was having dinner with clients and would have to get back to me. So, I called Luna before it got too much later in Atlanta. "Hi, Luna. How's it going?"

"You won't believe this!" she exclaimed.

"What?" I asked.

"Mom was blackmailing Lars. She mixed her martinis and meds again and spewed it all out. Get this: she doesn't really know anything, but he bought it and started handing out money, five grand at a time. All Mom knows is something about money and murder, if she even got that right. She doesn't know who, when, or why. She's coming on like she knows more to get Lars to cough up the dough. She said it was easy money and she thought she might as well benefit while she could, but now that she knows her brakes were tampered with and she almost died, she's really scared."

"Your mother has no filter on her actions or her mouth," I declared. "She might want to consider returning the money and admitting that she knows nothing."

"That's an excellent suggestion," Luna concurred. "I doubt she'll do it, though. Mom loves her nips and tucks and expensive clothes."

I hung up and wandered over to talk to Jaime, who answered the door and handed me a cosmopolitan. "I was just coming up to get you," he said. "Chris made a pitcher of cosmos. We thought we'd sit in the garden."

I checked on Mom, who was still napping, so I went out and plonked down in a chair, lifting my Cosmo with a salute to Chris. "These are delicious, Chris."

"Thank you. My bartending job in my college years has paid off. I'm a better bartender than I am an engineer. Why I picked engineering as my major, I'll never know."

"Because that was 'the major' at that time. Just like communications was 'the major' when Kat went to Cal. Sociology was 'the major' when I went to college, but I chose English lit because it was my true love. And, Chris, you engineered yourself into owning the most popular hair salon and spa in Santa Monica."

"True. And I do adore hair styling. It satisfies my creative outlet."

Turning to Jaime, I said, "This week off has been a little slice of heaven: sleeping in, shopping, and going out to lunch. I feel like I'm in The Housewives' Club with some of my friends: playing tennis, shopping, lunching, getting facials and massages. I could get used to this. However, I need to pay the bills and bank some money. So," I continued, "we're busy in the next few weeks. That's a good thing. What's on the schedule?"

"Well, the Johannsen firm has a new case on the books. It looks like a class-action suit. They've scheduled lots of depos. We may need to get help from your court reporting collegemates, Mary and Andrea."

"Sounds good. Mary is in Venice Beach now, and Andrea bought a duplex in Westwood, so they won't have to traipse over from the Valley and worry about the traffic on the 405."

Mom came out, and Chris handed her a Cosmo. We talked about the upcoming Halloween parade, of which Jaime is the organizer. Santa Monica residents love their parades, and Jaime loves putting them together. Eventually, we all got hungry and decided to check out a new restaurant on Wilshire Boulevard. It was a lovely, peaceful evening in my beloved Santa Monica with some of my favorite people. But as I got ready for bed, I couldn't help but wonder about Missy and her blackmailing. What was that girl thinking? How much does she really know?

Chapter 19: Nine Minutes
Friday, October 18, 1996

It was a beautiful morning. I checked in with Jaime and went for a run. When I got home, my phone was ringing. It was Mom. "Good morning, honey. Did you have a nice run?"

"Yes, it's lovely down in Palisades Park. The sun on the water makes the ocean waves twinkle. How are you this morning?" I asked.

"I'm great! Since you're off work today, I thought it might be nice to go to the Malibu farmers' market. What do you think?"

"I think that's a splendid idea. Give me thirty minutes to shower and change, and I'll come down and collect you."

"Okey dokey! See ya in a few," Mom said.

It was a good thing I brought our little farmers' market cart, because we ended up buying more than we could carry. I bent over to arrange stuff in the cart, and when I straightened up, I quite literally bumped into Dixie, knocking her cup of tea right out of her hand.

"Dixie, I'm so sorry. Thank goodness you had a lid on it, so it didn't spill all over. Let me buy you another one."

"No, no. It was just as much my fault, and I'm done with it anyway. How are ya doin'?"

"I'm great," I answered. "I was off this week, and it's been marvelous. I could easily find myself a luxurious member of The Housewives Club— although, my tennis game is a bit rusty. How about you? How's it going with Lars?"

"Well, business with him has slowed down a bit. He's had some problems at work, and get this: Mrs. L. finally got up the balls to kick him out. He's actually livin' in the condo he bought for me downtown, and I'm back in my little place in Santa Monica. The gossip is that Mrs. L. has a lover. I say, good for her. It's about time. And, let's face it, my business will never slow down."

Laughing, I retorted, "How true! You chose a fail-proof profession. I'm happy for Mrs. L., too. She deserves better than Lars. I'd better find Mom and get this stuff home. We'll talk again soon. Take care."

"You too. See ya!"

***

Back at home, I helped Mom in with her groceries, then took mine up and got them put away. I made a cup of tea and took it out to the garden with a Carolyn Hart mystery. Carolyn's Annie Darling series has always been one of my favorites. Before too long, Jaime came out with a Hardy Boys mystery.

"Getting back to your childhood, are you?" I joked.

"Actually, I'm rereading it in an attempt to get back to the basics. I decided to write a mystery

122

about a court reporter's assistant who solves mysteries, but I'm spending more time staring at the screen than writing."

"Oh, Jaime, you're funny!"

"We'll see how much you laugh when I'm a famous mystery writer. Maybe I'll let you come with me to my interview with Oprah." We giggled and quipped back and forth, and couldn't stop laughing.

After about an hour, I announced, "I'd better go get cleaned up. I'm taking Mom out to dinner before Friday night services. What are you guys up to tonight?"

"Chris put something in the slow cooker this morning. Whatever it is, it smells divine. I taped a few episodes of *Cheers*, so we'll watch those after dinner. "

"I love *Cheers*! Have fun. I'll see you tomorrow."

When I got upstairs, I had a message from Tommy saying that, indeed, the security tapes showed that Baxter had been missing for nine minutes and thirty-eight seconds—long enough to use the restroom, but would it be long enough to alter brakes?

***

We arrived at shul early, so we had time to greet friends before we found a seat. Mrs. L. was there with Norma, but for the first time I can remember, Lars was not at Friday night services. He was probably too embarrassed to show his face. He always holds himself out to be so sanctimonious.

As it turns out, it wasn't embarrassment that kept him away.

We heard the sirens during the service. Now, in Los Angeles sirens are a normal happening, especially in the Valley where police helicopters are a common occurrence, but in sleepy little Santa Monica, not so much. People began to squirm and look about. I told Mom to sit still, I'd go out and take a look. Outside, Eighteenth Street was blocked off by two police cars and an ambulance. A man was lying in the street being attended to by paramedics. I saw Officer Newsome and walked over.

"Hey, Newsome, what's happening?"

"Addie! Gosh, I'm not on duty. I was coming to services myself, running late as usual. Lars was ahead of me, dashing to get across the street before the walk timer went to red. A black Mercedes sped up and swerved, looking like it was intentionally trying to hit Lars. I yelled at the driver to watch out. He must have heard me and swerved the other way. He gave Lars a pretty good bump, but he didn't kill him, as he probably would have had he hit him head-on. Even with my training, I was so intent on watching Lars and shouting at the driver that I didn't get an ID. It all happened so fast."

Lars was trying to stand up, so the paramedics walked him over to the emergency vehicle and sat him down. I told Newsome I'd see what I could find out. I walked over to Lars and the paramedics.

"Lars, it's Addie. Can I help in any way?" Lars stared at me with a blank look.

"He's in shock. It doesn't appear that he has any serious injuries, but we're going to take him over to the ER to be on the safe side. Are you family? A friend?" one of the paramedics asked.

"An acquaintance. But his wife is inside attending Friday night services. I'll let her know what's happened."

"Okay. Thanks."

Services were over by the time I got back inside. I couldn't find Mrs. L. Mom said she and Norma left right after the service ended. I couldn't help but wonder if that hit-and-run wasn't an accident.

Chapter 20: The Frying Pan
Saturday, October 19

I had a nine o'clock tennis game with my friend Krazy Kathy. Kathy and I met when I was working at the phone company and going to college. She got the nickname Krazy Kathy because there aren't too many pranks she wouldn't try to pull. Many years ago, when we were at the Playboy Club in Hollywood, she lifted some bunny ears off the end of the bar and stuck them on her head. The Playboy Bunny had momentarily set them down while repairing her hair. When she turned around to put them back on, they were gone. Krazy Kathy is very fast. The Bunny was looking all over for them—everywhere but on Kathy's head. I caught her eye and pointed to Kathy. When the Bunny saw them on Kathy's head, we all started laughing.

I arrived a few minutes early and saw that Kathy was already out on the court. "Hi, Kath! How are you doing?"

"Hi, yourself. I'm good. How's the reporting business?" Kathy asked.

"Well, I ended up being off this week," I replied. "It's a long story. I'll tell you all about it over lunch. Kath, I haven't played tennis in years."

Kathy is married to a rich film producer and has plenty of time to play tennis.

"I know. That's why I got you out here," she laughed. "First, I'll win. Second, you've got to get out more."

"I know," I admitted. "I started online dating. I've had one date with an eighty-two-year-old gentleman."

"What?" Kathy laughed.

"Yeah. He lied about his age. I was shocked," I said. "He was a pleasant enough guy, though. It wasn't a bad evening. I have another date tonight."

"Oh, goodness! Why don't you hire one of those matchmakers?" Kathy suggested.

"That's not a bad idea," I admitted. "I just might do that and cut through a lot of the preliminaries."

We played a few games, cleaned up, and had lunch at the Jonathan Club restaurant. We ordered a bottle of pinot gris and club salads. I filled Kathy in on Jonesy's death, Missy's accident, and the events following.

"Addie, your job is so exciting. I live vicariously through you," Kathy declared.

"Oh, goodness, Kath, you don't want murder and mayhem crossing your path. You're the one with the exciting life, going to all those exotic locations for filming."

"It is an extraordinary life, that's for sure," she agreed. "I'm very fortunate."

Kathy's first marriage hadn't been so charming. Her husband consistently cheated on her, and her daughter died from complications of anorexia.

Since Missy suffers from bulimia, Kathy and I are devoted volunteers for the Eating Disorders Hotline.

We finished lunch around two o'clock and said our goodbyes. Kathy lives out in Calabasas, so she had to hit the road before the traffic gods condemned the freeway. I stopped at the drugstore to pick up a prescription of latanoprost for Mom's eyes. I passed Ye Olde King's Head, a specialty shop that sells English foods, condiments, and various strictly British items. I couldn't resist running in to purchase a few things. We all like to keep the meat pies in our freezers for that occasion when nothing else suits.

I arrived home with just enough time to get ready for my online date. He wanted to meet at four o'clock at the cowboy beer bar up on Topanga. My friends and I used to go there in our college days to listen to music that was so loud the seats vibrated. I knew my jeans and cowgirl boots would be perfect. It had begun to rain, so the roads were wet, which can make it tricky going over Topanga; however, when we were teenagers, Dale had taken me up to the canyon to teach me how to drive, so I knew every turn like the back of my hand. I found parking easily enough.

As I walked by the windows of the establishment, heading toward the front door, I saw only one person inside, an older fellow in a leather jacket sitting at the bar with his back to me. He had thinning, dyed red hair of various lengths that stuck out all over his head, and he held a beer in each hand. He turned his head slightly and I saw he was at least in his seventies, on a good day. My first thought was, *Oh, no, no, no, I can't do this*. But not wanting to be rude, I went on in. "Hi! Brady?"

"Yes, ma'am! You're sure a pretty little thing. I'll just bet you're my date, but if ya ain't, ya are now."

"Uh, yes, I think I might be. Are you from the online dating service?"

"Oh, yes, ma'am. An' I sure got lucky this time. You're one real hot babe. Let me buy you a beer."

I thought, *Jumpin' jupiters! How did this happen?* But, I said, "Could you excuse me for a minute? I need to use the ladies' room."

"Ah, sure, honey," he said. "You go right ahead. I'll order that beer and a couple more for me; I'm a two-fisted drinker. Ha! Ha!"

I went toward the restroom, out the back door, jumped in my car and drove down Topanga toward home. I felt a little bit guilty about leaving the guy hanging, but the guilt wasn't bad enough to stop me from driving. And, as it turned out, that wouldn't be the worst thing that happened to me that night.

***

It was only 5:30 p.m. when I arrived home, but being October, it was already dark. I pulled Mini into the garage, got out of the car, and started for the side door leading toward the cottage. I thought I'd see if Mom's day had been any better than mine. Suddenly, an arm in a black shirt grabbed me from behind and shoved me to the ground. I was winded but nothing was broken, that I could tell.

He wasn't a big guy, but he was strong. However, I'm strong, too. I lurched up, but I only got as far as my knees before he pushed me back down. I started yelling for help, and that's when he put his dirty, smelly hand over my mouth. I thought I was going to puke.

"Be quiet and stay calm, and everything will be all right. I only want that envelope. Where is it?" he demanded.

His hand came away from my mouth. I wanted to bite it, but I was afraid I would get some rabid disease and die a slow, painful death.

"I don't know what you're talking about. What envelope?"

"You picked up an envelope in a deposition at the Larceny Law Firm last week."

"No, I didn't."

"Yes, you did."

"Did not."

"Did too. Listen, bitch, I don't have time to play games," he said. "Where is it?"

He bent my wrist back so far, I thought it would break. I screamed bloody murder. He slapped me across the head, causing my ears to ring. All I could think was that if he broke my wrist, I wouldn't be able to report. Then I thought, *but I have great insurance.* "All right. All right. Stop twisting my wrist. I'll get it for you," I said.

Suddenly, I heard a thwomp, and the guy fell on me real hard, pushing my face into the cement. At least he let go of my wrist.

"Oh, my poor baby chick! Are you alright?"

It was Mom. She rolled him off me, and slowly I got to my feet. Mom stood with a frying pan in her hand. The guy was on the ground, knocked out cold. There wasn't any blood, which I suppose was a good thing.

"Mom, are you okay?"

"I'm fine. My arm might be a little sore tomorrow, but this shithead is going to wish he'd never come around here." Raising her arm, she said, "I'm going to hit him again just to make sure he's out for a while."

"No, no, Mom. It's okay. You saved the day. I love you."

I became all verklempt and gave her a huge hug. Then I called 911 and Brent. While we waited for them to arrive, Mom told me she'd heard me drive in and then scream, so she grabbed her frying pan and ran out the door to the rescue. The paramedics arrived as the man in black began waking up.

Brent and a couple squad cars arrived and took over. Mom brought out some Halloween cookies and took coffee, tea, and water orders while I gave my statement. I had no idea what envelope the guy was talking about. All my exhibits are checked by me and then again by Jaime, and we'd found no envelope. They identified the man in black as John Smith—very original name—but the guy wasn't talking. Mom gave a short statement, and soon enough everyone was gone. We let out big sighs of relief, and Mom stated, "I think it's a double Manhattan night."

I agreed, and we went into the cottage to mix them up. We took them out to the garden and toasted to life. We talked about the envelope. What's in it? What could it say? What could have happened to it? Why does John Smith think I have it? Why does he want it? Does he work somebody? If so, whom? Our minds were spinning. The questions came endlessly.

Finally, Mom said, "Hey, I forgot about your date. How did that go?"

"Oh, Mom, you wouldn't even believe," and I went on to describe my latest date. After some good laughs, which we desperately needed, we decided to go on down to the Broken Drum, our go-to place for dinner. While we were enjoying our second Manhattans and dinner, Brent called me on my mobile.

"Hi Addie! John Smith called his attorney. Guess who? Three guesses and the first two don't count."

"Don't tell me it's Lars," I blurted.

"Right on," Brent confirmed.

"That can't be a coincidence," I stated.

"Not likely. I'm being paged. I'll call you tomorrow."

Chapter 21: Family History

Sunday, October 20, 1996

The next morning, I felt like a football in a losing game. I called Chris to see if he could possibly get me in for a massage appointment any time that day. He and Jaime had been out with friends the previous night, so I had a lot of explaining to do. He got me in for a massage at 11:30, and as it was only ten, I went down and sat in the hot tub for a while, hoping to alleviate some of the discomfort my body was in at the moment.

The massage was heavenly and righted some of the damage to my poor body. When I got home, Kat called, and we talked for an hour and a half. It was so nice to catch up on what she was doing. She and her granddad—my dad—are very close. She's his go-to person for everything, so I caught up on what he'd been doing as well. It had been a while since I'd spoken to him, and I realized I should give him a call. He'd been in New Zealand consulting on a helicopter museum being built there.

Dad was the expert everyone wanted when it came to helicopters. He was a test pilot for Bell Helicopters back in the early '50s. In 1954, he flew the first helicopter into California to start an ambulance service. Later he advocated for heliports. In the mid '60s he opened his own flight school,

The Helicopter Center, at the Van Nuys Airport. He operated it for twenty years, then let his manager take the reins and finally sold it to him last year. Since he turned the business over to his manager, he'd been doing consulting work all over the world on anything helicopter-related—and, more often than not, fixed-wing as well. Sometimes, when her schedule allows it, Kat accompanies him, and on occasion, Dale or I do as well.

On Monday, I had a 10:00 a.m. depo at the Mason McClintock firm on Wilshire. I like to have my equipment ready to go the night before, so I checked everything: DataWriter, tripod, cords, exhibit stickers, etc. Everything was in order. I just had to put my laptop in my bag in the morning. At 5:30, I saw Mom, Jaime, and Chris out in the garden with cocktails, so I pulled a bottle of Grgich chardonnay out of the wine cellar, grabbed a couple glasses, and went downstairs to the garden. They had the fire pit going, and the earthy smell of woodsmoke intermingling with the salty ocean air gave me a sense of peace. "Hi, guys! How's everything?"

Jaime piped up first, "The big question is, how are you? Did you take ibuprofen? Did the massage help?"

"Yes, to the ibuprofen and the massage. I'm still sore, but I think a glass of this lovely chardonnay will complete my recovery. It's still a mystery why anyone would think I have an envelope. And what's in the darn thing anyway?

Mom, how are you doing? Does your arm hurt from swinging that frying pan?"

"My arm's okay," she replied. "I took your advice and iced it before I went to bed last night.

"I talked to Missy today. She has to go in for another surgery, and needless to say, she's not happy about that. Luna left and Sunbeam arrived. She'll probably be there for the duration of Missy's recovery, since she doesn't have a job. Frankly, I think she doesn't want to work. I've financed bartending courses, massage school, cosmetology, and personal training. Neither she nor her mother ever finish anything they start."

Jaime said, "Well, Vesta, you did the best you could with Missy, and you did a good job of getting Luna through college. Missy is a law unto herself, and Sunbeam honors her mother by being just like her. For goodness' sakes, we couldn't even talk them into getting their GED. They think school is a place to get pregnant. Sometimes you just have to let go and let be."

I changed the subject to the upcoming Halloween parade. "Jaime, how are the arrangements for the parade coming along?"

"Oh, you know, the usual, figuring out who gets to do what, when, where, and how. They get competitive about it, and sometimes downright ruthless, but in the end, everyone has a good time. However, it is exhausting. Every year I say I'm not volunteering to be in charge again and yet I do. I actually have a fabulous committee, so everything is just falling into place. Our dear friend Iris lends sensibility to the project, and Krazy Kathy adds lots of crazy."

"What outlandish costume do you have planned for this year?" I asked.

"I'm not telling, but it will be quite scandalous, I can assure you of that."

"How about you, Chris?" I added.

"Oh, you know me. I like to repeat my childhood costumes: The Lone Ranger, Tonto, Huckleberry Hound, Superman, Gumby, Captain Kangaroo, Sheriff John. I'm rather conservative compared to our Jaime."

"Mom, you and I get to ride on one of the floats again. Who or what will you come as?"

"I'm thinking about being a heroine and waving my frying pan around," she laughed.

Jaime jumped in, "I think you should wear your mink again. Last year was a hoot when that animal activist started throwing tomatoes and yelling at you for wearing fur, and then you caught a tomato, threw it back to her and shouted, 'Sweetie Pie, you're wearing leather shoes.' She clearly wasn't expecting that. She had no retort. Maybe you should come dressed as a tomato this year in case she returns."

Mom chimed in, "That reminds me of the time Missy went to the parade as Snow White. She rode in the float with your dad's helicopter and insisted on sitting in the pilot's seat. She'd been sneaking candy all day and threw up all over the cockpit. Your dad was so angry. He wanted to send her off to boarding school in Ely, Cambridgeshire, near my mum and dad. I almost agreed, but I didn't want to put that sort of pressure on my mum. She was getting up in years and having the pressure of an errant child nearby would have done her in."

My mother's parents were from London. My grandfather attended medical school at Cambridge, and my grandmother owned a boutique there. They met at The Eagle, a famous pub in Cambridge. They got married and honeymooned in New York, where my grandfather eventually took a position at the St. Francis Hospital in Flower Hill. They loved it there, but when my grandfather retired, they decided to go home to England and purchased a beautiful five-bedroom home in Ely. I have so many delightful memories of visiting them in Flower Hill and Ely. They're in their early nineties and still enjoy their tea and cocktails and, of course, their truly amazing gardens. They have season tickets to the Royal Opera House and often get over to Stratford-on-Avon to enjoy some Shakespeare.

Chris said, "So, do tell, Addie, what will your costume be?"

"I have not a clue. Oh! I know. How about Brenda Starr, Ace Reporter?"

"Very apropos, darling."

We laughed and carried on for a while longer, but we soon went our separate ways for dinner. I had a bowl of pumpkin soup and went to bed early. I dreamed about Gabe. I saw him in the fog, but I couldn't reach him. A beer floated out of the fog, and I grabbed it. Suddenly, I sat straight up in bed, startled and off kilter. I'd heard something. Law and

Order were curled up on the bed, so it wasn't them getting into mischief. What was it? I walked around the house turning on all the lights and examining every nook and cranny but found nothing amiss. Was I going crazy? No one could get in this house; my security system is the top of the line. I let out a huge sigh and crawled back in bed, cuddling up with Law and Order and telling the universe, *No more dreams, please.*

Chapter 22: Suspicious Circumstances
Monday, October 21, 1996

The deposition at the McClintock firm was a new case and involved two attorneys I wasn't acquainted with. One was from Chicago. His plane was late, so we had to wait two hours for him to arrive. The other attorney was fresh out of law school and new to the McClintock firm. He seemed like a nice kid. It was a wrongful termination suit. A woman from Human Resources was our witness. She didn't mind the delay because she was basically getting paid to sit and read a book while we waited. I didn't mind the wait either. There was always something to do.

Since I was caught up on my proofing, I walked down to the knitting shop in the next block and soaked up the woolly smell of all the yummy yarns. It was a little slice of heaven. I pored through patterns and pulled out balls of yarn, trying to decide which one to match with what pattern. I finally decided on a pullover vest in a soft cotton yarn in varying shades of brown. It was an easy project, so I also picked out something a little more challenging, a complicated pattern for a cardigan with a sky-blue cashmere yarn. I paid for my purchases and headed back to the office, stopping for a latte and almond poppy seed muffin to take with me.

We still had an hour before counsel from Chicago was due to arrive, so I found an overstuffed chair in the lobby and folded myself into it with one of Lillian O'Donnell's mysteries, *Don't Wear Your Wedding Ring*. I'd picked it up at Once Read Books in Long Beach and was anxious to delve into it.

An hour later I was startled out of a chase down an alley when counsel said, "Ms. Henkey?"

I jumped up. "Oh! I'm sorry, Counsel, I was so wrapped up in this mystery that you caught me off guard. Please call me Addie, by the way."

"Must be a good book," he said.

"Yes, it is," I replied. "Lillian O'Donnell was one of the first authors to introduce a female police officer as a protagonist. It's quite a captivating story. Are we ready to begin?"

"In about ten minutes. Opposing counsel just arrived and needs a few minutes. And please call me Andy."

"Okay, Andy. I'll be right in."

Ten minutes later, I introduced myself to counsel from Chicago. "Hi! I'm Addie Henkey, your reporter for today."

"Nice to meet you, Addie. I'm Roger Stephens. Here's my card. We're going to want this transcript expedited for Thursday. Will that be okay?"

"Absolutely," I exclaimed.

I swore in the witness, a pleasant but also very nervous gal of about forty. It's often quite intimidating having to give testimony in a court case. I gave her a big smile and took a deep breath, hoping to relax her. She'd been in charge of Human

Resources for about three years and kept meticulous records, most of which got entered into evidence.

The gentleman who thought he had been wrongfully terminated appeared to have a history of slacking on the job: coming in late, leaving early, smoking marijuana in the men's room, and falling asleep on the job. Plaintiff and Counsel Stephens claimed the marijuana was for medicinal purposes. The testimony droned on. I was in danger of falling asleep, and the witness was fading, so I called a break at three o'clock. "Excuse me, Counsel," I interjected at an appropriate time, "I think we could use a short break."

"Of course. I'm sorry, I should have done that an hour ago. Let's take twenty minutes."

I typed in, "Off the record at 3:11 p.m."

"Would you like some coffee?" I asked the witness. "I happen to know where the break room is."

"Oh, yes, please," she responded.

"Follow me," I said.

As I was pouring coffee, I received a call from Norma on my mobile. "Hi Norma! What's up?"

"Lars wants a copy of the police officer's depo in Expert Doc's drunk driving case expedited for tomorrow morning. Can you do that?" Norma asked.

"I sure can. Tell Lars it will be on his desk first thing in the morning." I was almost grinning.

As our witness stirred cream into her coffee, she said, "I don't mean to pry, but was that Norma from Mr. Larceny's office?"

"Yes," I replied. "Do you know her?"

"Boy, do I ever," she exclaimed. "She left our firm under very suspicious circumstances. It seems she—"

Just then, Andy walked into the coffee room and asked, "Are you ladies ready to reconvene?"

"Yes, we are," I replied.

Back in the conference room, we started up again, and the deposition continued. It wasn't the most tantalizing testimony. At six o'clock I finally heard my favorite words: "I think that's it for today. Thank you, everyone. We can go off the record."

I wanted to speak to our witness, but she jumped up and was on the lobby phone before I could waylay her. I decided to watch for her to finish her call and catch her then.

While I collected all my exhibits and packed up, I addressed Andy, "Roger asked to have the transcript expedited for Thursday. Would you like your copy then, too?"

"Oh, yes, thank you," Andy replied. "And I almost forgot—Counsel Hamish, who is representing Plaintiff's manager, wasn't able to attend today, but he asked me to order a copy for him as well. Here's his card. You can check with his office about getting it expedited."

Oh, how I love multiple copies and expedites. Cha-ching, cha-ching! I looked through the glass doors out to the lobby. Our witness was nowhere in sight. Dang!

***

I arrived home at 7:15. The neighborhood was lit up with more outdoor Halloween decorations. People were really getting into the spirit. Before I dragged my equipment up the stairs, I went over to the cottage to check on Mom. She saw me coming, "Hi, sweetie! How did it go today?"

"A very boring wrongful termination case. How was your day?"

"Oh, I had a wonderful day," she exclaimed. "Jaime gave me a ride to Chris's for an eleven o'clock hair appointment. Then Chris took me to lunch. Then the pedicurist had a cancellation and asked me if I'd like to get a pedicure. I couldn't say no to that, right? And that's why I'm wearing Zoris in October. Then as I was waiting for my toes to dry, my friend Betty was just leaving and sporting a new hairdo. She asked me if I wanted to take a run over to Saks to see the new collection of holiday dresses. I couldn't say no to that, so off we went. Of course, we hit traffic on the way home, so I just got in twenty minutes ago. I opened a bottle of Kendall-Jackson chardonnay. Would you like a glass?"

"I'd love one. Thanks, Mom. Our witness today told me that Norma left the last firm she worked for under suspicious circumstances. We didn't have an opportunity to continue our discussion because we were reconvening the depo. Darn! I'd love to know what that was all about. I think I'll try to sneak it into a conversation with Norma. Anyway, we got a late start this morning, so that gave me time to run into the knit shop over there, and I left with two new projects. I brought them in to show you."

Mom oohed and aahed over my yarns and we chatted away while sipping wine. "Iris brought over a very large container of her jambalaya first thing this morning. Would you like some? It should be heated enough by now."

"Are you kidding me? Iris is the best cook in Southern California. Of course, I want some. Let me run my equipment upstairs and change out of this suit. I'll be back in twenty minutes."

I spent a lovely evening with Mom, enjoying her company, eating jambalaya, and watching an old Doris Day movie. I got home about eleven, sent my job off to Patrice, and climbed into bed with Law and Order and Lillian O'Donnell's book. I couldn't keep my mind on the mystery, though, because I was thinking about another mystery: What had Norma been up to?

Chapter 23: Theatrics
Tuesday, October 22, 1996

I was all set up for my nine o'clock depo at the Sprekleman law firm in Century City and was working with my favorite videographer, Scott, who was also ready to roll. The attorney for the plaintiff, and the plaintiff himself, were present. He was suing his longtime girlfriend, and business partner, over a dissolution of the business. The defendant walked in ten minutes late.

My mouth dropped open. She was one of the most beautiful women I'd ever seen; tall, long-legged, with chestnut-brown hair flowing over her shoulders and deep-set, burnt umber-brown eyes. She wore a gorgeous Yves Saint Laurent black suit. It had a pencil skirt and a very low-cut jacket. She also wore a beige silk blouse and beige Gucci stilettos. It took only a few seconds for her to spot the plaintiff, whereupon those beautiful brown eyes flew wide open and she heaved her Louis Vuitton handbag across the room, missing the plaintiff and hitting Scott's camera, which tumbled over as Scott groaned and dropped to the floor to recover his equipment.

The woman screamed obscenities at the plaintiff. She had the mouth of a truck driver.

She took off her high heels and hurled them at the plaintiff. He ducked and laughed uproariously.

Counsel for the plaintiff shrieked, "Get your client out of here, now."

Counsel for the defendant was yelling, "Your damned client is an evil, cheating bastard."

I reached in my briefcase and grabbed a gavel I keep for occasions like this. I banged it on the table, shouting, "Quiet, please, all of you."

People began to realize the absurdity of what was taking place, and counsel for the defendant, who was closest to the door, began to gently ease his client out into the lobby. Counsel for the plaintiff asked his client to follow him to his office. Suddenly the room was quiet. I dropped down in my chair.

"Good grief!" I said to Scott. "Is your equipment okay?"

"Yes," he responded, "thanks to this highly padded carpeting."

We were both too stunned to say much more. I picked up the defendant's shoes and handbag and walked out to the lobby, where she and her counsel were conferring. I handed them to her without saying a word. She took them, and putting on her shoes, she said, "Thank you. I'm very sorry for the ruckus. That man has ruined me financially and has the gall to sue me, the bastard. I hope he rots in hell."

"Meanwhile," Counsel said, addressing his client, "do you think you can continue with the deposition if the plaintiff agrees to leave the room?"

"I don't know," she answered. "I wasn't expecting him to be here. He really gets my dander up."

No kidding! I thought.

Counsel proposed, "Let me talk to his attorney and see what we can arrange. Why don't you go down to the café and have a cup of tea? See if you can calm down."

Counsel walked down the hall and Defendant strode toward the elevators. I returned to the conference room. After about twenty minutes, counsel for the plaintiff came in to tell us that we would resume in a few minutes, minus Plaintiff's presence.

Half an hour later, I swore in the defendant, who appeared overly calm. I thought perhaps she'd had a bit more than tea during the break. A couple hours later, we broke for lunch. I'd brought a salad, and I was starving, so I gobbled it right up while I worked on the transcript, cleaning up the spellings of names and unusual terminology. I took a stroll, did some stretches, and soon everyone was back in the conference room ready to resume.

***

The afternoon was uneventful, thank goodness. It was a sad case of two people who were once in love and had been business partners. Now they were breaking up not only their relationship but their business as well. I was happy when we adjourned at four o'clock.

I decided to stop at the Louise Green Hat Shop on my way home. A little retail therapy was just what I needed. I parked and climbed the stairs of the old Victorian, feeling very much like a lady of that era. A new hat at that time would lift a woman's spirits, and I knew just how that felt. I tried on nearly every hat in the store because I was having fun and I loved them all. I settled on a frilly orange fascinator with black velvet trim. Grandma Hammersley, Mom's mom, from whom I get my fascination with hats, would love it. I was taking Mom to her bridge ladies' Holiday Tea at the Rendezvous Court next month, and this would be the perfect hat to wear.

***

With my hat stop, I didn't arrive home until 6:30. I could hardly wait to show Mom my new hat, so I went straight over there. I tried it on for her.

"Oh, my! That is lovely, isn't it?" she exclaimed. "You look stunning. You'll be the envy of the tea party."

"Thanks, Mom. We must send pictures to Grandma Hammersley. I'm exhausted. My depo today was quite unusual, to say the least. Come up for a glass of wine and I'll tell you all about it. I put a roast in the crockpot this morning, so let's have that for dinner."

"Sounds delicious," she replied. "Give me about twenty minutes."

I took everything upstairs, changed into comfy lounging clothes, and emailed today's job to

Patrice. Mom and I spent a pleasant evening together gabbing about anything and everything. I opened a bottle of a pinot noir from King Estate in Oregon and filled her in on my crazy morning. The roast was delicious. I swear, everything I put in that crockpot is outstanding. We watched a few old episodes of Perry Mason. Mom adores Della Street's sling-back shoes and gorgeous 1950s-style suits. I walked her over to the cottage around 10:30 and gave her a hug goodnight. When I returned home, I couldn't get into my pajamas fast enough. I was asleep as soon as my head hit the pillow. I dreamed about a man in black wearing an orange fascinator and drinking tea.

Chapter 24: The Mercedes

Wednesday, October 23, 1996

I drove to LAX, parked the car and went to greet Dale as he exited the airplane. We both had big, silly grins on our faces. He dropped his briefcase and grabbed me in a big bear hug.

Every woman within sight was looking our way, absolutely stunned by my brother's captivating presence. We picked up his luggage, retrieved Mini, and headed for PCH, laughing and chatting all the way to his house.

"I'm really looking forward to your big Halloween bash on Saturday night. What can I do to help?"

"Bring Mom, Jaime, and Chris and be at my house at five o'clock. I scheduled the party for six o'clock, so that will give us a few moments to have some alone time and catch up on our lives. And wear an outrageous costume. Pete and Thelma have everything else under control."

"Of course, they do."

Pete and Thelma are retired Army. Pete was a court reporter in the Army, and Thelma was a cryptographer. I met Pete at a court reporters' conference in Honolulu twelve years ago. Thelma had come along for the fun of it. Dale and Annie were staying at their condo there and invited us all over for dinner. We became fast friends, and when

Annie got sick a few years later, Pete and Thelma moved into the mother-in-law wing of the beach house to help out. They remained with Dale after Annie died. I don't know what my brother would do without them.

As I backed out of Dale's driveway, a black Mercedes pulled out of the driveway next door, so I hesitated, allowing whoever it was to go ahead. When the car didn't move, I pulled out. I was going to stop at a new law firm on Santa Monica Boulevard to drop off some business cards and let them know that we'd be happy to do their depositions.

I was only about five minutes from Dale's when I noticed a black Mercedes behind me. Was the car from the neighbor's driveway following me? I told myself not to be so silly. There must be thousands of black Mercedes in Los Angeles. A few minutes later, the Mercedes was riding my bumper. The driver continued riding my bumper all the way to the law firm.

As I parked Mini, the Mercedes pulled ahead and parked in the next block down. I entered the ornate doors of the new law firm and asked for the person who scheduled depositions. I was directed to Mrs. Smythe, a pleasant woman in her sixties. She offered me coffee, and we had a very lovely chat. I left her with our rates, and she promised to call and set up a deposition with us.

As I was pulling Mini out of my parking spot in front of the law firm, a black Mercedes suddenly appeared from nowhere, coming straight at me. I laid on the horn, which must have startled him because he swerved, just missed me, and hit the car parked in front of mine. My heart beat a mile a minute.

People ran out of the law firm and other nearby businesses. The Mercedes backed up, hitting an oncoming car, and raced down Santa Monica Boulevard, swerving in and out, and barely missing other cars. The receptionist from the law firm rushed up to me.

"Are you alright?"

"Yes," I assured her. "He just missed me."

I stepped out of Mini and realized that I was shaking like a leaf. I grabbed a coat from the back seat and put it on. I gasped when I looked around and saw what a mess the Mercedes had left behind. The passenger side of the Chevy in front of me was caved in. The car in the street had been hit in the front. The driver stood beside his Lexus, looking stunned. Two squad cars pulled up. Two officers went to the driver of the Lexus and two approached those of us standing on the sidewalk.

"Does the Chevy belong to someone here?" asked one of the officers.

No one claimed it, so I spoke up, "It was hit by a black Mercedes. I wasn't able to identify the driver because the car windows were heavily tinted. The license plates were smudged with dirt, so I was unable to get the license plate number."

"And your name?" the officer asked.

"Addie Henkey," I answered.

"Can you tell me what happened, Addie?"

"Yes. I was just beginning to pull out into traffic when the Mercedes came barreling down on me. I laid on my horn. I think that startled the driver, and he ended up hitting the Chevy. Then he backed up, hitting the Lexus, and took off speeding down Santa Monica Boulevard, weaving in and out of cars. Thankfully, he didn't hit anyone else that I noticed."

Addressing the people standing around, the officer asked, "Did anyone else see what took place here?"

No one came forth.

"Can I get your driver's license, Addie?"

"Sure." I reached into the car and retrieved my license from my wallet, handing it to him.

"We'll list you as a witness on the accident report. Is this your current address?"

"Yes."

"Can I get your telephone number?"

I gave him the information. Paramedics had arrived and were talking to the driver of the Lexus, who pointed at me. The paramedic approached me, "Ma'am, do you need medical attention?"

"No. Thank you. I wasn't hit, just shook up, but I'm okay."

Just then, the owner of the Chevy came rushing out of an office building. When she saw her car, I thought she was going to throw up. "Omigosh! What happened?" she exclaimed.

The officer spoke up, "I'm sorry, ma'am; your car was run into by a hit-and-run driver. No one was able to get an ID on the vehicle, other than it was a black Mercedes. May I see your driver's license?"

Shaking, she reached into her purse and handed the license to the officer. "I'll need a copy of the report for my insurance company."

"Certainly," replied the officer. "Let's see if your car is operable." Turning to me, he said, "Addie, if you'll move your car, it will be easier to get her car out, and you can leave. If we need anything more from you, we'll be in contact."

"Thank you," I said. People had begun going back into their offices and shops.

As I drove home, I replayed the car crash scene in my head. Was the Mercedes really coming right at me? Maybe he lost control of his car. Why would someone want to crash into me? Was it the same vehicle that was riding my bumper?

Chapter 25: Poison
Thursday, October 24, 1996

I woke up at five o'clock. Going back to sleep didn't appear to be an option, so I took a cup of coffee back to bed with me and proofed transcripts until the sun came up. I changed into my running clothes and ran down to the Palisades, working in a little Fartlek training, which is basically switching between faster sprints and recovery periods. As I slowed down and came up the walk, Jaime was at his front door. He spotted me.

"I was just coming to look for you. Would you like to report a two o'clock doctor depo?"

"Sure. Why not," I answered.

"It's your favorite expert doc," Jaime said with raised eyebrows.

"Don't tell me it's Lars's Expert Doc," I retorted.

"One and the same," Jaime said. "It's just at the Smart Firm down on the Venice Boardwalk, so you have plenty of time."

"Great!" I exclaimed. "Email the info to me."

"You got it," Jaime confirmed.

I went over to the cottage to say good morning to Mom. "Good morning, sweetie," she greeted me as she opened the door. "I just hung up from talking to Dale. He wants to take us out to dinner before services tomorrow night."

"Wonderful! I'm in. I just picked up a two o'clock depo down on the Venice Boardwalk. I think I'll go over there early and look around Small World Books."

"Oh, I want to come. I'll hang out in the shops while you take your depo."

"Wonderful! How about we leave around 11:30?"

"I'll be ready," Mom declared.

***

I hate Venice parking lots. They're grossly over-crowded, but the valet promised to take good care of Mini. "Mom, I'm going to take my equipment up to the law offices and set up. I'll meet you in Small World in fifteen minutes."

"I'll be there."

***

Fifteen minutes later, I was wandering around the bookstore with Mom. I found a signed first edition of *The Stories of Ray Bradbury*. I purchased it as a gift for our childhood friend Richie. His birthday was coming up, and he planned to come down from Seattle to stay with Dale for a few days. He collects Bradbury, and I was pretty certain he didn't have this one, since I'm usually the one who finds them for him. I saw Nevada Barr's new book *Firestorm* and picked that up. I noticed that they also had a copy of *The Fallen Man* by Tony Hillerman, so I put that in my basket for Dale. Mom and I met Nevada at the Left Coast Crime (LCC) conference earlier in the year, and we'd met Tony Hillerman last year. Dale joined us for that one. He also loves to read mysteries and attends the conferences as often as he can. LCC is a conference that's held once a year for fans of mystery fiction. It's so much fun to meet your favorite authors, hear them talk about their writing, purchase their books, and then have them sign their books for you.

Mom had several books in her basket, including Sue Grafton's new book *"M" Is for Malice*, which I was also anxious to read. I paid for my purchases and left Mom perusing books with the agreement that she would meet me at the law firm at 3:30. I was pretty sure this depo wouldn't go too long.

***

"Do you solemnly swear or affirm to tell the truth, the whole truth, and nothing but the truth?" I asked, as I administered the oath to Expert Doc.

"Yes," he replied. I doubted that he could tell the truth, very often at least. He was testifying about poisons and how they might affect the body. "This particular one," he said, pointing to a photo—I typed in, "Witness drawing attention to a photograph marked into evidence as Exhibit 3"— "the poison in question," he continued, "would make the person appear fatally poisoned; however, it is expelled from the body within twelve hours."

The light bulb went off in my head. OMG! I wasn't a Valley Girl, but I sure did pick up the lingo. I'll just bet Expert Doc poisoned himself.

Holy Toledo! He wanted to make it look like Lars poisoned him. He's trying to get rid of Lars. Suddenly, I realized I'd missed the question Counsel had asked.

I interrupted. "I'm sorry, Counsel, but my brain skipped a beat, and I missed your question. Could you repeat it, please?"

Counsel's infamous answer was, "I'll try."

The depo went on, putting me in grave danger of falling off my chair out of boredom. Finally, I heard the words I adore: "That's it for today. Thank you, Counsel. Thank you, Expert Doc. And thank you, Madam Court Reporter."

"Off the record at 4:02 p.m.," I typed in.

Poor Mom. She's been waiting for half an hour. I wandered into the lobby and there she was, ensconced in an overstuffed chair, reading a book, and sipping a glass of wine.

"Well, I see you made yourself comfortable," I said, startling her.

"Oh, my goodness, Addie, you surprised me; I was so immersed in Sue's new book." Yes, Mom was on a first name basis with Sue Grafton. "The lovely young receptionist offered me a glass of wine. How could I refuse?"

"You couldn't," I laughed. "It would have been rude. Give me ten minutes to pack up my equipment. Say, while we're down here, why don't we have a cocktail at the Candle Café?"

"Oh, that sounds wonderful. I'll leave the wine. It wasn't exactly top shelf."

***

Half an hour later, I'd put my equipment and our book purchases in Mini, and we were sitting in the Candle Café enjoying Manhattans and a calamari appetizer.

"You know," I said to Mom, "I think Expert Doc may have poisoned himself in order to throw suspicion on Lars. He testified about poisons today and, in particular, one that is discharged from the body within twelve hours. Doesn't that sound familiar?"

"Good grief! Wouldn't that be rather dangerous? What if it backfired? He could have died."

"I know, that thought occurred to me as well. I guess that's why he's called Expert Doc. He's also very cocky and self-assured. He probably thinks he couldn't go wrong. I need to mull this over, maybe run it by Brent."

"That's a good idea," Mom concurred. "I talked to Missy today."

"Oh, she called?" I asked, surprised.

"Are you kidding? No, I called her. Missy never initiates a call unless she needs money. At any rate, she had another surgery and is doing well. She's up and moving about a bit. She's still in an abundance of pain, though. I feel guilty for not going back there and helping out, but our lives are so peaceful right now, I do not want to get inundated with drama. It's too exhausting."

"I know. Dale said the same thing. And, of course, I feel as both of you do. None of us wants the drama back in our lives. Dad and I spoke recently. I suggested family therapy, and he said he was on board. Now to convince Missy."

"Good luck with that," Mom countered.

We ordered dinner and continued chatting. It was ten o'clock by the time I got home and sent my transcript to Patrice. She'd sent me some proofing. I printed it, but wasn't about to begin reading it tonight. Rather, I cuddled in bed with Law and Order, my book, and thoughts of poison spinning around in my head.

Chapter 26: A Slap in the Face

Friday, October 25, 1996

The morning brought rain to water the gardens. The air smelled fresh of moisture and damp soil. I love rainy days. Mom didn't want to miss her bridge game, so I put on my Hunters, the "in" rainboots at the moment, and drove her over to Mrs. Carlson's house on San Vicente.

Mom's bridge partner was going to bring her back home, so I was pretty free for the day. Patrice had sent me some more proofing; therefore, I needed to get home and get that done, but I was low on some cosmetics, so I popped into Nordstrom's. As I was picking out what I needed, I caught sight of a wheelchair being pushed up to the counter beside me. I glanced over, and there was Baxter pushing the wheelchair.

"Mr. Baxter, hi! I'm Addie Henkey, the reporter on the deposition where you jumped across the table and started choking Attorney Jones."

"Oh, yes, I remember you. I was so embarrassed about choking Mr. Jones. I've been under tremendous pressure trying to take care of Mom and fighting that lawsuit."

The very attractive older lady in the wheelchair spoke up. "My son wouldn't hurt a flea. That was just a real bad time. My name's Sally, by the bye."

"It's nice to meet you, Sally. I see we both like Lancôme cosmetics."

"Yes, I love them," she said. "I've used Lancôme for years. It's so nice to be out and about again. Right now, I need to use the wheelchair for outings, but it won't be long before I can store it in the garage. I'm working with a real nice physical therapist, who's doing wonders with me. And he's easy on the eyes, too, if you get my drift."

I laughed, "That's certainly an added benefit."

Sally continued, "At home, I manage on my own quite well. That subacute nursing facility was a horrible place. They kept me there drugged up and flat on my back just to cash in on Medi-Cal funds. Think about it: $20,000 a month from the government, just for my care. Multiply that times several hundred patients. As soon as my son confronted them about keeping patients there to collect government money, I was suddenly improved and able to go home five weeks later. What a racket. My son's an accountant, and he looked carefully at the invoices. That's how we discovered that doctor padded his bills. He said he gave me tests and things that he never did. When I told him I didn't get those tests, he said I had dementia. I wanted to smack him. I'm as sharp as a tack."

"You've been through a very rough time, Sally. I'm sorry."

"I'm lucky to have such a wonderful son. He's been my advocate. If it weren't for him, I'd still be in that awful place."

Baxter spoke up, "I was very sorry to hear about Mr. Jones's accident. He was a decent guy. It's that Mr. Larceny that's the crook. The world would be a better place without him. I heard he and his expert doctor are great pals. Two peas in a pod, I'd say."

The cashier had rung up my items, so I paid for them and said my goodbyes, wishing Baxter and Sally lots of luck.

I spent the afternoon listening to the sound of the rain against the windows and getting caught up on my proofing. I sent the final transcripts down to Jaime to bill out and send to the law firms. It was four o'clock. Dale was picking us up at five o'clock, so I had just enough time to shower and change clothes.

***

We enjoyed a delicious dinner at Valentino's. Handel and Newsome happened to come in at the same time we arrived, so we all sat together, catching up on our lives and the case at hand. We talked about the Halloween party for the next night. Nobody dared reveal what they were wearing. We didn't want to ruin the element of surprise. I posited my theory about Expert Doc poisoning himself to throw suspicion on Lars. That idea got tossed around the table as a bit bizarre, but, as I like to say on occasion, stranger things have happened. We all agreed Lars was callous, devoid of character, and contemptible.

We arrived at shul early, allowing Dale time to greet friends and share his adventures working with

Uncle Bud. We found seats near the front and next to Mrs. L. and Norma. Lars came in late and sat in the back. After services, we filed into the all-purpose room for the Oneg Shabbat. Everyone appeared to be enjoying themselves, sipping beverages while they chatted. Dale adored Cantor Cohen and was deep in conversation with him. Mom and I are co-chairs of the Membership Committee, so we were speaking with a family that had recently joined the synagogue.

Lars and Mrs. L. were having a heated conversation, gesturing and pointing their fingers in each other's faces. Their conversation was getting louder and louder. Lars's voice was high-pitched as he said, "You're just a sick old lesbian. No wonder you're so awful in bed."

"You're a lying, conniving cheat. You cheated on me with your whores, and you cheat on your clients. I'm surprised you're still in business. You won't be for long," Mrs. L. yelled.

"What would a f'g lesbian know about a law firm?" he retorted.

"I'd rather be a lesbian than married to an asshole." She hauled off and smacked him so hard he spun around. His face was red, and he looked like he was about to pass out. Mrs. L. is a large woman, and Lars is a small man. Norma tugged at Mrs. L's arm, and Cantor Cohen walked Lars out of the room.

Mom addressed the new family members, "I'm so sorry. This has never happened before. I hope you won't think badly of us."

Mrs. Gold, of the new family, assured her they would not. "Things happen that are out of our control," she said.

Isn't that just the truth, I thought.

Chapter 27: The Party

Saturday, October 26, 1996

I succumbed to the luxury of sleeping in. I'd fed Law and Order before going to bed last night, so with full tummies, they were on board with sleeping in, too. I went for my run, cleaned up, made coffee, checked on Mom, and took my proofing into the living room by the fireplace where I'd be comfortable while I worked. Law and Order made themselves cozy by the fire, and there we sat until just past noon when Mom came to the door with a bowl of freshly made squash soup.

"I knew you would be working most of the day and thought you might need some sustenance," she said. "I just tried this recipe. I think it's my best."

A few months ago, a friend had invited us for lunch and served squash soup. Mom hates anything that smacks of vegetables, but in an attempt to be polite, she'd tasted the soup and discovered she loved it. She's been on a squash soup kick ever since. Fortunately, it's one of my favorites.

"This is delicious, Mom."

"Thank you. How does it compare to the other recipes?"

"Oh, goodness. I'd have to do a taste test of the soups at the same time, you know, like wine tasting, because I can't remember from week to week.

Although, I have to say, there hasn't been one I've disliked."

"Oh, that's good. I like this one with that little hint of cumin in it. I'd better let you get back to work and go get my kitchen cleaned up."

***

Suddenly, it was three o'clock. I had just enough time to put on makeup and get dressed for Dale's Halloween party. I was going as Nancy Drew. I copied the outfit she wore on the jacket cover of *The Secret of the Old Clock*: a navy-blue suit with the skirt falling just below the knee, a light blue silk blouse, a paisley scarf in blues and browns, a navy-blue cloche hat, and brown shoes with a medium heel and a strap across the instep. I couldn't carry around a clock, so I chose a magnifying glass instead.

Dale was sending over his driver to pick us up at 4:30. He'd insisted that we should all be able to have a few drinks and not worry about driving home. At 4:20 I went downstairs to meet up with Mom, Chris, and Jaime. I knocked on Mom's door, and Cinderella at the ball answered.

Mom took my breath away. "Mom, you look stunning. Where did you ever get that costume?"

"A friend of Newsome's just opened a costume shop on Santa Monica Boulevard. Great timing, wouldn't you say?"

"Yes, I certainly would say."

We walked over to Chris and Jaime, who were waiting in front of the garage. Jaime was dressed as one of the Hardy Boys. He sported brown slacks and a blue cashmere pullover sweater with a brown-and-blue plaid collar sticking out. "How did you know I was coming as Nancy Drew?" I asked.

"I had no idea. I've been rereading the Hardy Boys books in preparation for writing my mystery novel, and it just seemed like the perfect Halloween outfit. I must say, though, great minds think alike. We're even color-coordinated." I looked over at Chris and saw that he was dressed as Prince Charming to my mom's Cinderella.

We were all having a good laugh as our driver pulled up, jumped out, and opened the door, first for Mom, then me, then Chris and Jaime. We settled into the luxury of the limousine. There was a bottle of sparkling wine chilling for us, but the drive to Dale's was only seven blocks down to the beach, so we decided to hold out for martinis at Dale's. There are only three parking spaces in front of Dale's garage; therefore, he'd made arrangements with the Jonathan Club for his guests to use their parking and catch a shuttle back down to his house.

After getting Mom out of the limo, as gracefully as we could in her Cinderella gown, we went into the house and Dale greeted us as Davy Crockett, one of his favorite childhood characters. He wore the soft leather pants with the pullover top and moccasin boots from, I was pretty sure, none other than the new costume shop in town, but the highlight of his outfit was his original childhood coonskin cap.

"Little Brother, you look amazing. I love, love, love your coonskin hat."

Mom chimed in, "Have you two saved everything you've ever owned?"

"Almost," Dale laughed.

"Mom," I said, "we know you still have our baby clothes."

"Well, of course," she retorted, "and didn't you enjoy using them when Kat was a baby?"

"I sure did," I confirmed.

"Speaking of Kat, how is she doing?" Dale asked, as we headed for the back patio overlooking the ocean.

"She's great," I answered enthusiastically. "She absolutely loves her teaching position and the campus. She bought a house in Lake Oswego that we must all go check out very soon."

"Yes," Dale said, "let's go visit her for Thanksgiving."

"I love that idea," I said, giving him a big hug. "And I know Kat will, too."

Pete and Thelma came in carrying a pitcher of martinis and glasses. Pete was dressed as Jeeves, Bertie's English butler from the P. G. Wodehouse books; and Thelma as a turn-of-the-century English maid. She wore a long white apron over a longer black dress with a small white lace collar. We all jumped up and began hugging one another. Thelma and Pete poured martinis, and we toasted to this extraordinarily fantastic family that we'd created.

Guests began arriving, and the house filled with the sounds of joy and laughter. Dale is so kind and welcoming. He invited his friends, my friends, Mom, Chris and Jaime's friends, coworkers, and,

I'm sure, some people he'd only just met yesterday. There were open bars on both levels of the house, and one on the patio where people could sit under outdoor heaters or warm themselves around a fire pit. Dale had Halloween movies playing continuously in the upstairs bonus room. There was a best costume contest: first place, a ticket to a showing at the Music Center, went to Kelly's hot new boyfriend, who dressed as Marilyn Monroe in her pink glam outfit from Gentlemen Prefer Blonds; second place, dinner at Spago's, went to Handel, who came as Lurch from the Addams Family; and third place, four tickets to Disneyland, went to Dale's paralegal, who came as Tinkerbell. I'm sure the new costume shop made a killing on this party.

I wandered into the game room, where people were crowded around playing Jack O' Lantern Can Bean Bag Toss, Halloween Skee-Ball, and Halloween Spoon Game. I got in the line for the bean bag toss right behind Appel, but I didn't recognize him dressed as the Lone Ranger, mask and all. He spotted me, though.

"Hi, Addie. Love your costume. It's so you. Say, we were both popular in the same time period, so it looks like the Lone Ranger and Nancy Drew could go out to dinner one night. What do you think?"

"Appel, that's reaching," I said, laughing, "but, Nancy Drew accepts your invitation."

"Great! The prize for dinner at Spago's reminded me that I haven't been there in ages. How about I give Puck a call and see if he can get us in next Saturday night?"

"You've got yourself a date, Mr. Lone Ranger."

"Addie, I've finally found you," said Whoopi Goldberg, a.k.a. my friend Iris. "How are you doing, darlin'?"

"I'm fantastic, really. It's so good to see you," I said, giving her a big hug. "You've been gone a long time."

"Ohhh, yes. You know my fear of flying. Well, I decided to take this course to overcome the fear of getting in an airplane. Your dad recommended it, by the way. They flew us up to Seattle for lunch, but I was so traumatized, I couldn't get back in the plane to come home, so I spent a week up there going to the theatre, sightseeing, and visiting friends."

"So, you finally got up the courage to fly home?"

"Oh, no, darlin'. I took the train home." We were laughing ourselves silly when another friend came along and stole Iris away. Before I knew it, the party was winding down. People caught the shuttle back to their cars.

Dale, Mom, Chris, Jaime, and I plopped down on the couch in the living room. "I'm partied out," Mom exclaimed, putting her head on Dale's shoulder.

"Me, too." I piped in.

Chris yawned and said, "I think I could sleep for a week."

The cleanup crew Dale had hired was busy taking glasses, plates, and leftover food into the kitchen. One of the crew, a young girl, came up to us. "Mr. Henkey, there's a gentleman in a Lone Ranger costume sound asleep out on the patio. I can't seem to wake him up."

"That would be Appel," I volunteered.

"Too bad we don't have our horns, whistles, and noisemakers from New Year's Eve," Chris said through a big yawn. Dale, Jaime, and I dragged ourselves out to the patio.

"Hey, Appel," I said as I shook his shoulder. "Poor guy. With his partner on vacation, he's been working some long hours. Appel, let's get up." I gave him a little tug, and he fell forward. "Oh my gosh. He's really out of it," I said.

I set him back up in his seat and removed his mask, but it wasn't Appel. "Who is this?" I asked Dale.

"That's Keith. He's one of my new associates."

I gave Keith a little pat on the cheek, but he wasn't responding. "I think something's wrong," I added, as I felt for a pulse.

"He's probably just passed out," Dale spoke up. "I don't think he's much of a drinker, so the alcohol probably hit him hard."

"We wouldn't know anything about that, would we?" chimed in Jaime.

"Guys, I can't get a pulse. Dale, you try. I'm going to run in the house and call 911," I said.

"The poor guy is going to have one mean hangover," Jaime added.

Dale exclaimed, "I can't get a pulse either. Let's get him down on the floor. I'm going to try CPR."

I was just inside the house on the phone in the living room. "We know where the old Kniss house is. We'll be there in a flash," the operator bellowed. I heard sirens as I hung up.

"I'm going to make sure the driveway is clear," I yelled out the door to Dale and Jaime.

The limo was the only car in the drive, so there was plenty of room for the paramedics. I waited there for what seemed like hours but, in reality, was less than ten minutes. As they pulled into the driveway, I shouted, "He's in here."

We all ran through the front rooms to the patio, where the paramedics took over for Dale.

"He's gone," they exclaimed almost immediately.

"Criminy! How could this possibly happen?" I cried.

Dale and Jaime put their arms around me. Stunned, we slowly sat down on the patio sofa. "I just spoke to him a couple hours ago," Dale said. "He was fine. He wasn't drunk."

Jaime brought out a pitcher of water and glasses and began pouring water for everyone. Mom and Chris came out to the patio.

"What's going on?" Chris jumped in.

"Keith is dead," Dale told him. "He was a new associate at my offices."

"Are you serious?" Chris cried out.

"I truly wish I weren't," Dale muttered.

Police cars stopped in front of the house, and Mom went to let them in. I heard one of them ask if the prince was at home. The last one in said "Hey, Vesta, I'd recognize you anywhere. How are you doin'?" It was Fred, probably the oldest officer on the SMPD and an old friend of Dad's.

"I'm good, Fred," Mom replied, "but our guest out on the patio isn't quite so good. One of the paramedics just pronounced him dead."

"Oh, geez, Vesta. I'm sorry. What happened; do you know?"

"No, we don't. He was seemingly young and healthy."

They walked out to the patio. "Addie, Dale! I haven't seen you two in a month of Sundays. You're both lookin' good. How's your dad? Travelin' all over I hear, making more money than God, and havin' fun to boot," Fred said.

"Fred!" Dale answered, getting up to shake his hand. "I'm so glad you're here. Yeah, Dad's great. We've got a terrible situation here, though. This young man, Keith, is dead. One of the cleanup crew found him and thought he'd fallen asleep. She tried waking him, but he wasn't responding, so she came in and told us. We went out to the patio, and Addie tried to rouse him, but he tumbled over. We couldn't get a pulse, so Addie rushed in to call 911, and I started CPR. The paramedics came in and pronounced him dead."

"Not a good ending to a Halloween party," Fred responded.

"It's quite grizzly, isn't it?" Chris added.

"So," Fred asked, "how did you guys know this fella?"

"He's one of my new associates. I invited everyone from the office to the party," Dale answered.

"At first we thought it was Appel because he was also dressed as the Lone Ranger," I spoke up.

"Appel?" Fred asked.

"Yes," I replied. "He's the plaintiff's attorney on a case against Larry Larceny. Jones, who worked for Larceny, had me doing his depos until he was killed in that car crash up on Topanga a few weeks ago."

"I heard about that crash," Fred said. "What a shame. Such a young fella."

"Wait a minute!" I exclaimed. "Keith and Appel were both dressed as the Lone Ranger. Maybe someone meant to kill Appel but killed Keith by mistake."

"So, you see a connection here?" Fred asked me. "Two lawyers, Jones and Appel, working on the same case."

"It just occurred to me," I muttered, thinking.

"However, we don't know that there's been foul play here," Fred said. "Though this fella is young, he could have died of an aneurysm. Guy next door to me was standin', talkin' to his wife, and dropped dead on the spot. Turned out it was an aneurysm. Now my wife's on my ass to retire before I drop dead. At any rate, we'll get a report from the pathologist. I'll let you know what it says. I'm sure sorry I had to miss the party. I was on duty tonight, but, judging from the mess, it looks like a good time was had by all—except, of course, Keith. I'll be in touch."

"Thanks, Fred," Dale responded, as he walked the officers to the door, with the paramedics wheeling Keith out just in front of them.

"I just bought a bottle of Uncle Nearest 1856 Premium Whiskey. Never tried it before. The cleaning crew will be here for another hour at least. Let's break it open. I could use a nightcap. Anyone else?" Dale asked. We all agreed that was a good idea.

***

It was three o'clock in the morning when the limo driver dropped us off at home. Chris walked Mom to her door, and I raced upstairs to bed. I was exhausted, but I tossed and turned for hours, dreaming of the Lone Ranger. He had a twin, and they had their Colt .45s pointed at each other. Suddenly, it was foggy, and they weren't visible. A shot rang out. I was walking in blood, when I heard a shout: "Hi Ho, Silver!"

Chapter 28: Mistaken Identity
Sunday, October 27, 1996

I slept till eleven o'clock in the morning. Law and Order must have sensed it had been a late night and left me alone while they bathed themselves and lounged quietly at the end of the bed until I stirred. I woke up feeling worn out. I couldn't believe that poor, young attorney was dead.

I threw on my shorts, shirt, and running shoes and headed down to Palisades Park, hoping to shake out the sadness and lethargy. I ran all the way down to Dale's. His surfboard was gone, so I knew he was out catching some waves. I walked down to the beach looking for him. I caught him riding a huge wave all the way in. I gave him a standing ovation.

"What's up, Big Sis?" he laughed.

"I woke up feeling so down in the dumps. I thought a run might shake it out, and I ended up here. I can't believe Keith is dead. I wonder what was wrong with him. I know he was new to your firm, but did he mention any health issues to you?"

Dale grabbed his board, and we walked back up toward the house. "No," he said. "He appeared to be a gym rat: weightlifting and cycle classes. He used the building's workout facility on his lunch hours. I never saw him taking any meds or recreational drugs. He drank, but not excessively."

"It's sad. Life can be cut short so quickly. It's scary." I didn't want to speak of Annie or Gabe.

"Yes, Ads, it sure is," Dale acknowledged. "Hey! Let's change this day around. Go home, get cleaned up, grab Mom, and we'll go to the Aero Theatre to see Mission Impossible."

"That's a great idea," I exclaimed. "See you in a few." I gave him a big hug and raced out the door, up to Palisades and back home. I knocked on Mom's door and told her Dale was taking us to the movies. I rapped on Chris and Jaime's door, too, but they weren't home.

***

Walking out of the Aero after the movie, we spotted Baxter and Sally. I introduced them to Mom and Dale.

"Baxter is suing Lars for the mishandling of Sally's Medi-Cal case and unnecessary subacute nursing facility treatment. I've taken a number of depos in the case."

"Yeah," said Baxter, "we go to court next week, and I wish the bastard would drop dead."

I changed the subject. We chatted about the movie for a bit and then went our separate ways. We walked over to Father's Office, a popular pub on Montana, and enjoyed burgers, beer, and fries. Mom and I decided to walk home and enjoy the beautiful Santa Monica evening, so we gave Dale hugs and kisses and sent him on his way.

***

My phone rang as I walked in the door. It was my brother. "Hi there! Haven't seen you in ages," I kidded.

"I had a message from Fred when I got home," Dale said. "Keith was poisoned."

"Blimey!" I replied. "Who would poison Keith and why? And how, actually?"

"It would be easy to slip something in someone's drink," Dale commented, "and, as you suggested, it could have been mistaken identity."

"So, if someone wanted Appel dead, he has something and/or knows something that somebody wants kept under wraps."

"That's a lot of somebodies and somethings, but it sums it up," Dale said.

"I can't believe a guest at the party would poison one of the other guests," I stated. "But anyone could have come off the beach dressed in costume, chatted up Keith thinking he was Appel, caught his attention elsewhere, and slipped him the mickey."

"I'm going to give Appel a call and tell him to watch his back," Dale said. "It sounds like someone might be after him."

***

I was in bed by 9:30, hoping tonight would be more restful than last night. I had an early depo tomorrow and wanted to be bright-eyed and bushy-tailed. People are unpredictable, so you never know what the next depo will bring.

Chapter 29: The Note
Monday, October 28, 1996

I arrived at the Mason McClintock firm at 9:15. I like to get to my depos early to set up my equipment and get all the info I need into the computer. I brought up the caption page and put in the title of the case, case number, etc. Then I entered all the information for the appearance page—attorneys' names and anyone else who might be sitting in—and set up shortcuts for unusual names and jargon, so by the time we began the depo, almost everything would be coming up in real time on my computer screen. If an attorney wants to hook up their laptop, he or she will see all the questions and answers on their screens as the words are being spoken. I like it when they want this service because we charge each attorney separately for it. I love reporting, but I also love the money that comes with it.

We took a nice long lunch break, so I was able to get all my exhibit descriptions on the exhibit page and do a lot of transcript cleanup. At the end of the day, I was done in. I began packing up my equipment. I pulled out a folder that I like to keep exhibits in, and out fell an envelope. I didn't equate it to the missing envelope the man in black was after until I opened it up and read, "We know you killed Hank Gould, and we're coming for you when you least expect it."

I sat down hard. Someone wants this envelope badly enough to almost kill for it. I called Brent at SMPD. He'd left for the night, so I paged him. He called right away, "Addie, what's up?"

"You won't believe what I just found," I declared.

"The envelope?" Brent asked.

"Dang! You're good. Yep. It was stuck in my large exhibit folder. I have a large folder I use when I get a lot of exhibits and a smaller one for only a few exhibits. This is the first time in a couple of weeks that I've had to use the larger one. It had to have gotten in there when I gathered up the exhibits at the Baxter depo. I'm racking my brain trying to think how it could have gotten mixed up with the exhibits, though. Oh my gosh! I know!

"Norma brought in an envelope for Lars when we were packing up to leave. She handed it to him, and he casually opened it while he chatted with Jonesy about the depo, but all of a sudden, his eyes flew open like he'd just been stabbed with a knife. At the same time, his mobile began ringing and he laid the envelope down while he fumbled around in his pockets, looking for the phone. The call distracted him, and he must have left the room without grabbing the envelope. Exhibits were all over the table, so I unwittingly swooped up the envelope when I gathered the documents."

"Well, now we know who's being threatened, but not by whom," said Brent. "Let's hope Norma remembers who left the envelope. Meanwhile, can you drop that off at the station on your way home? Handel is on duty tonight."

"Of course. I have to tell you, though, my fingerprints will be all over it, as well as Norma's and Lars's. You've got my fingerprints on file, but I don't know about Norma's and Lars's."

"Handel will check. Good work, Addie."

"It was purely accidental. I'm leaving, so I'll drop this off in about twenty minutes."

"Watch your back. Lars still doesn't know where that envelope is, and we can't pick him up on that note alone."

"I'll be fine. I've got Mom and her frying pan on my side. Talk to you soon."

Before I left the law office, I carefully used a Kleenex to drop the envelope into a folder so that I wouldn't get any further prints on it. At the station, I personally handed it to Handel and gave him a brief explanation of what happened. Pulling into my garage, I gave a good look around to make sure there were no men in black lurking in dark corners. The coast was clear.

I got my equipment bag upstairs, which isn't an easy job because it's heavy. I should install an elevator, but it's an expensive proposition. Law and Order greeted me with disdain because I'd been gone all day. They like food, treats, and love on demand. They're quite spoiled little monsters. I gave them treats and got my own treat, a nice glass of chardonnay. Before I got too cozy, I went down to the cottage to check on Mom and found she'd had a good day on the phone gossiping with family and friends all over the country.

Mom is good at keeping in touch with people. Before Dad retired from the Navy, we moved around quite a bit, but Mom never left a friend behind. I have cartons of letters she saved. Mom wanted me to have them because Missy wouldn't understand the significance and would probably toss them out. They're a family saga extending over fifty years. When I retire, I'd like to write a novel based on the history in the letters.

I filled Mom in on how I found the envelope and dropped it off with Handel but warned her that we're not in the clear yet. Lars still doesn't know where the envelope landed, nor in whose possession it might be.

I went back to my office and sent my transcript to Patrice. Then I checked in with Jaime. I was going back to the McClintock firm tomorrow, while Mary and Andrea were lined up to handle other depos. I put a chicken breast in the oven, which brought Law and Order to the forefront. They know I'll share some of it with them, so they lie down in front of the oven purring while they wait for it to cook.

I got into my cozy loungewear and settled in front of the fireplace with a book, biding my time until the oven timer went off. The phone rang. A gentleman from Match.com wanted to know if I would be free to meet him for drinks at six o'clock tomorrow down at the Jonathan Club on the beach. I told him I'd take a look at my calendar and get back to him. I checked out his profile. He was a bit pudgy, but nice-looking, a businessman with several properties in the valley, and looking for love—of course, weren't they all. I called him back and told him that I'd see him at six o'clock tomorrow evening.

Chapter 30: Mini's Near Miss

Tuesday, October 29, 1996

The depo the next day was pretty uneventful except for the fact that the witness, a rather full-of-himself type gentleman in his sixties, kept winking at me. I finally stopped the depo and asked him if he needed a break because it looked like he had something in his eye. We finished up at 4:30, which gave me just enough time to get home and send my transcript to Patrice. I decided I didn't have time to change from my suit to casual attire, but that was fine. People often went to the Jonathan Club right from work.

I valet-parked my car and headed into the bar. I recognized my date right off. He looked just like his picture, which was refreshing. He'd secured a table off to the side of the bar. We greeted one another, and each ordered a glass of white wine. We chatted for a bit, and then he asked me, "Are you into group sex?"

I stared at him for a moment, making sure I'd heard correctly. "That's not really on my bucket list," I replied.

He took it quite well. We had some further polite conversation, and then he asked me if I'd like to have dinner. I said that would be lovely, but I had to get home and get some work done. I rescued Mini from the valet car park. She hadn't been moved yet, so the kid threw me the key, and I took off. I'd only gone a couple of blocks when I hit a red light, but I couldn't stop. I had no brakes!

My stomach turned over, my heart was pounding, I couldn't breathe. I dodged cars and sweat bullets. I turned left in front of a car coming toward me. He slammed on his brakes as I lurched onto the island in the center of San Vicente. I turned off the ignition. Mini was slowing down, but a tree loomed up right in front of me. I opened the door and rolled out onto the lawn. Mini came to a gradual stop within inches of the tree. I managed to get to my feet, wet from the damp grass and shaking in my stilettos, which had buried themselves in the dirt.

The man in the car that had come to an abrupt stop as I swerved in front of him pulled to the side of the road, turned on his flashers, and jumped out of his car, running toward me. "Are you alright?" he asked.

"I think so," I replied through chattering teeth. "I lost my brakes and couldn't stop. I'm so sorry."

"You're in shock. I have a blanket," he said, jogging back to his car and returning with a blanket that he put around my shoulders. The warmth enveloped me, and I began calming down.

"I think we should call 911," he stated.

"I don't think there's anything the police can do. There's no damage, other than a horrific scare. I'll call my Mini Cooper road service."

"Let me do that for you. Sit down on this bench over here. My name's Jon, by the way. And yours?"

"Addie," I replied.

"That's a beautiful Mini Cooper you have," Jon said.

"Thank you. It's pretty new, and I love it. I'm so glad it wasn't damaged. I feel like it's my kid."

He laughed. "I know just what you mean. I love my little Boxer."

The serviceman arrived promptly. He'd only been a few blocks away on another call. He said I was extremely lucky—like I didn't already know that—and that my car was in good shape. I didn't have any brake fluid, but he could fill it up, get Mini off the island, and I could continue on my way.

After the serviceman had gotten Mini onto a side street, he left, and Jon walked with me to my car. I handed him his blanket and he handed me his card. "I'd love to see you again, Addie, under more pleasant circumstances, of course. Maybe we could get together for dinner one night?"

I took his card and said, "Thank you. I'd enjoy that. I'll send you an email when I'm not wet and shaking."

At home I took a hot shower, and after a little more work on the transcript, I sent it off to Patrice. My mobile sang, "I'll take Manhattan, the Bronx and Staten Island, too..."—my ring tone for Mom because of her favorite drink.

"Hi, Mom. I got in a bit ago, but I had to take a quick shower. How are you doing?"

"I'm good. I played a game of tennis over at the Jonathan Club this afternoon, came home and got cleaned up, and now I'm experimenting with some cosmopolitan recipes. I saw you come in. I'll have a couple tasters ready for you in a few minutes."

"Sounds great. I'll make a quick call and be over in a jiff."

I'd been thinking that my brake fluid couldn't have been empty. Mini is less than a year old and she's been serviced recently. I called Brent to see what he thought, but he wasn't in, so I spoke to Handel.

"Hi, Handel. How are you doing?"

"Good, Addie. How about you?"

"Actually, that's why I'm calling. I had a bit of a scare on my way home tonight. I tried stopping at a light, but my brakes failed. I made a sharp left turn onto the island on San Vicente, turned off the ignition, and Mini came to a stop. The serviceman came out and said I didn't have any brake fluid. He filled it up, and everything appears to be fine. However, Mini was just serviced, so it doesn't make sense that I didn't have any brake fluid, especially given that Jonesy's and Missy's brakes were both tampered with."

"Where were you parked just prior to the accident?"

"I'd parked in the valet park at the Jonathan Club."

"Oh, geez! That's a busy lot."

"Yes, it is. They were so busy that Mini was the twelfth in line and hadn't been moved, so I just grabbed the keys and left."

"We're in luck," Handel declared. "I'm going to send someone out right now to see if there's any indication that your brake fluid was drained."

"If the brakes were messed with, then somebody still thinks I've got that note," I declared.

"Omigosh, Addie! You've got to be careful," Handel exclaimed.

"Yeah. Well, I was escaping a Match.com date and didn't think to check my brake fluid as I left. In fact, checking my brake fluid has never been on my to-do list."

"Whoever did this was probably wearing gloves," Handel speculated, "but we can dust for prints anyway. Can you bring your car in in the morning?"

"Sure, if you can give me a lift to my depo. It's just up on Wilshire. However, the serviceman will have his prints all over the car. You'd have to get him in as well."

"It's worth a try. I won't be in in the morning, but I'll leave a note for Brent," said Handel.

"Great. I'll be there eight o'clock-ish. My depo starts at ten. Take care."

"You're the one that needs to take care," Handel replied with concern.

"I'm in for the night. What else could happen?"
***

I walked over to Mom's and was greeted with cosmopolitan samples. "Thanks, Mom. These look great."

"They're two very different recipes for cosmos. What do you think?" she asked.

One was tangy and the other was sweet. Normally, I wouldn't go for sweet, but tonight I did. "They're both good, but this evening I'm leaning toward the sweeter one," I told her.

"I am, too." Mom said. "How did your date go?"

"Good gracious, Mom. I don't think this Match.com thing is going to work. He wanted to know if I was into group sex. Really!"

"What did you say?" she queried.

"What do you think I said?"

"I don't know. Nothing you do would surprise me."

"Oh, Mom. I hope you're joking. I told him it wasn't on my bucket list."

"Well, that's sort of non-committal," she stated.

"Non-committal? What the heck are you talking about?"

"It leaves it open," she proclaimed.

"Really? I never thought of it that way. Maybe that's why he asked me to stay for dinner."

"And you didn't?" Mom asked, astonished. "Dinner at the Jonathan Club is a treat. The last time I was there, Pierce Brosnan sat at the table next to me. What a heartthrob! He kept glancing my way. I couldn't keep my eyes off him all night."

"No wonder he kept looking at you. At any rate, group sex is not something I'm into, and I won't be seeing that guy again." I sipped my Cosmo. "There's something else I should tell you, because you're bound to find out anyway, but I don't want to upset you. Someone may have drained the brake fluid out of Mini while I was at the Jonathan Club. On the way home, I hit a stop light, but my brakes failed. I dodged a few cars and made an abrupt left turn onto the island on San Vicente. I quickly turned off the ignition, and Mini stopped just short of a tree.

"My abrupt left turn caused a very nice gentleman to come to a screeching halt. He pulled over and came to my rescue. I was a bit shaken, but without a scratch. He brought me a blanket and called Mini Service. They arrived in a timely manner, touched off the brake fluid, and I came home."

"Good grief," Mom said, with alarm.

"You might say. I just spoke to Handel. He's sending someone over to the valet park at the Jonathan Club to see if there's a puddle of brake fluid where my car was parked."

"Thank goodness for his prompt action," Mom replied. "He's such a sweet boy. Since neither of us has had dinner yet, let's go to the sushi restaurant on Wilshire. My treat."

"That sounds great," I exclaimed. "I'll go change clothes and grab a sweater."

"Likewise," she said.

***

After arriving home from a relaxing and delicious dinner, I walked Mom to her door and went up to my flat. I had a message from Handel. Indeed, there was a puddle of brake fluid in the vicinity of where my car was parked.

Chapter 31: Comedy of Errors
Wednesday, October 30, 1996

The next morning, I dropped Mini for fingerprinting, and Brent gave me a lift over to the McClintock firm with a, "Call me when you're done, and I'll pick you up."

The day went quite well. This was a class-action suit, so the depos could go on for months. The more depos you report in a case, the easier the job becomes because you develop a case-specific dictionary with all the players' names and unusual terminology. It almost reports itself. I was also working with Scott again, my favorite videographer. We'd been working together for years. One time, I arrived at a depo, and the trunk on my Jetta wouldn't open. Scott saved the day by going through the back seat into the trunk and retrieving my equipment.

At the end of the day, I called Brent. "Hi! I'm ready for my limo."

"Great. I'll be there in twenty minutes, give or take."

I called Mom but got her answering machine, so I left a message letting her know that Brent was picking me up, but I'd be home soon. I packed up my equipment, got the exhibits in order, and took the elevator downstairs. Brent was waiting. I jumped in the car and began peppering him with questions, "How did it go? Did you get any fingerprints? Do you have enough to arrest Lars?"

"We did get some prints," he answered. "The mechanic from Mini Service came down on his lunch hour and got fingerprinted. Tomorrow, we should be able to eliminate him and get a comparison on the other prints."

"Good news," I said.

I retrieved my car from the station and was home in no time. I lugged everything upstairs and called Mom. There was no answer. Where could she be?

I went down to the cottage. The door was wide open.

Panic-stricken, I raced in to see the place in shambles: pillows strewn about the living room, the frying pan lying on the couch, the office door broken and the window open with the screen pushed out. Outside the window, the bushes were crushed and broken. It looked like someone had rolled around in the grass. I ran back up to my flat to call Brent. As I grabbed the phone, it rang. "Hello! Hello!"

"I've got your mother. You know where I am. Bring that note here now. And no cops."

The police had the original note, but thankfully I'd retained a copy, which I retrieved from my office. I ran downstairs, jumped into Mini and took off. Topanga Canyon was only moderately busy, but still it was 7:30 when I arrived. The parking attendant was gone, so I self-parked. I left the note and envelope locked in my glove box, locked the car, and took the elevator up. The reception area was empty. I left the door open and cautiously looked around the lobby—but not cautiously enough.

Before I knew what happened, I was grabbed from behind. My arms were wrenched behind my back, and rope was wrapped around my wrists. I kicked my foot up behind me to wallop Lars in the groin, but he was taller than I, and I missed by a mile. I drove the heel of my stilettos into his instep as hard as I could. He screamed and jumped backward. He still had hold of the rope, which caused me to fall back into him. He staggered but stayed upright, while I hit the floor.

Something in my left shoulder popped, and I cried out in pain. Lars grabbed my left leg and dragged me across the lobby and into an empty office where Mom was tied to a chair and struggling to get free. A kerchief was tied around her mouth. Her eyes were taut with fear and dread at the sight of me being yanked across the floor. Lars tied me to a chair while demanding to know where the note was. Suddenly, I heard Mrs. L. coming into the office calling, "Lars, where are you?"

I started to scream, but before I could get a sound out, Lars jerked the monogrammed hanky out of his pocket and tied it around my mouth. He walked out of the room closing the door and calling, "I'm in my office. Come on down."

I banged the chair as best I could, but I couldn't move it enough for anyone to hear. I heard Lars in his office, though. Someone had left the intercom on. It sounded like Lars was pouring himself a drink. Mrs. L. said, "Oh, pour me one, too. It's just what I need right now."

While they had some nonsense conversation, I pulled on the ropes, trying to unravel them. I wasn't having much luck, but I had my Swiss Army knife in my new Brighton mini cross-body bag. I got the strap in my mouth and maneuvered the bag behind me. It took me several attempts, but I finally got it open. The bag is small and box-shaped, so I was able to hold onto it with one hand and fumble around inside the bag with the other. I just about had my fingers on the knife when I heard someone going down the hallway toward Lars's office.

"Norma, whatcha doing her'? Thought ya lef' fer t'day." Lars slurred his words.

"I did, but I returned with Mrs. L. You knew that Mrs. L. was Hank's fiancée and you killed him to marry her and get your hands on the money. What you didn't know is that Hank was my brother. Mrs. L. is the one who wrote the note, and she put a very heavy sedative in your whiskey. We'll give it a few more minutes to take effect. Then we're going to take you for a little ride. Your brakes will fail, just like Hank's and Jones's. We've waited many years to avenge Hank's murder. We didn't know how it happened until his body was found and I heard you and Expert Doc talking," Norma replied. She took a huge intake of breath and gasped, "My water just broke. The baby, she's coming."

Mrs. L. sounded excited. "We've got to get out of here. Lean on me. Everything is going to be all right. I love you, Mon Cherie. I'll get you down to the car. The hospital is only a few minutes away."

They left the offices. I wasn't too worried about Lars; it sounded like he'd passed out—but then I heard his chair scraping the floor. *Ugh!* He was still moving. I grabbed the knife, but it slid back into my purse.

Suddenly, Baxter's voice came from nowhere, booming, "Where are you, you son of a bitch? I'm going to kill you, asshole." Footsteps echoed down the hall and into Lars's office. "You're nothing but a con artist. You nearly killed my mother. She was in that horrible nursing facility for a year. You kept her there for the money. Now you're turning things around and winning this lawsuit with your lying and cheating." It sounded like he was choking Lars, and Lars was struggling to breathe.

Then there was a lot of commotion out in the elevator lobby area. Baxter and Lars became quiet. The commotion in the lobby intensified. What the heck was going on? Baxter said, "Shit! Someone's coming. I've got to get out of here." His running footfalls quieted as he passed down the hall and out of the offices through the door to the exit stairs.

Two women were walking down the hall laughing and giggling, "Larsy, baby, where are you? Are you hiding on your little puddin' pies? We know what you like, sweet pumkin'. We're wearin' pasties with thongies and garter belts with the black sparkly hose you like and the black diamond-studded stilettos you bought us. Where are you? Are you wanting to play a little hide and seek? Come on

196

out now, ya hear. We're all hot and ready for Mr. Pleasure. There you are, you silly. Whatcha doin' on the floor? Are you playing possum on your favorite gals?"

One woman gasped. The other woman was screaming, "Good lord, Rosie! He's not moving. Maybe he's dead. We've got to get out of here, now." With their stilettos clicking loudly on the tile floor, they ran down the hallway and out the door.

Finally, I got the knife in my hand, but I was having trouble cutting my ropes. I scooched my chair closer to Mom and began sawing away at her ropes.

Someone else came running through the lobby, yelling, "Wher' ta hell are ya, ya cheatin', lyin' scum piece of shit? I'm na goin't live in fer of gettin' caught an' longer. I told ya I wanted out. Ya wouldn't listena me. Now I gotta kill ya, douchebag."

It was Expert Doc. He was drunk and slurring his words, stumbling down the hallway, banging into the walls. We didn't hear anything from Lars. It appeared he was still passed out. Expert Doc entered Lars's office yelling, "Ya shoulda let me out, asshole. I tried to kill ya by hittin' ya with my car, but some jerk yelled at me and I missed, but this time I ain't missin'."

A gun went off several times. Glass shattered and water gushed out of what must be the alligator tank. "Oh, no!" Doc yelled.

We could hear him as he kicked and slopped around in the water. There was what sounded like a rip in fabric. The Doc screamed bloody murder. "Shit! Ta gator got ma pants!"

Lars's office door slammed shut, and Doc ran down the hall and out of the office. I got Mom's ropes cut. She had a hard time standing up after being tied down, but she managed and got my ropes undone as well. We ripped off the hankies covering our mouths and grabbed each other, hugging.

"Mom! I'm so sorry. Are you hurt anywhere?"

"Just stiff. And I imagine Lars is, too. It wouldn't take those alligators long to gobble him up."

I grabbed a phone and dialed Brent. He answered on the first ring. "Get to Lars's offices now. He's been drugged, and he's locked in his office with the alligators on the loose."

"Jesus! I'm on my way. Don't open that door, Addie."

***

Mom and I sat on the leather sofa in the reception area, hugging each other. I love my mom so much. I came far too close to losing her tonight, and that scared me. Within what seemed like minutes, Brent and four officers came rushing out of the elevators with a medical response team.

Right away Brent began admonishing me, "Sufferin' succotash, Adeline! What are you doing here? If anything happened to you and Vesta, I couldn't live with myself, and Dale would kill me. Just because you had a little job in high school working for SMPD does not make you a trained police officer. Why didn't you call me before coming over here?"

Avoiding that question, I replied, "Speaking of my brother, we'd better give him a call or he'll be madder than all get out when he finds out what happened."

"I'll call him," said Brent, "but you're not home free; I want to know why you didn't call me. You can't just go running around doing crazy things and putting your life in jeopardy."

"Sorry, sir, but we need to get these ladies' vitals," one of the medics interrupted. They proceeded to take our pulses, our temps, look into our eyes and ears, and make sure nothing was broken. They put my arm in a sling to rest my shoulder and told me to get it X- rayed as soon as possible. Mom had begun to shake, so they bundled her in a warm blanket and asked if she wouldn't like to go to the ER to be checked.

"Not on your life, buddy! Been there, done that, and it took me a year to escape," she said. She was, of course, referring to the ER visit we made a few years back, which ended with her in a subacute nursing facility.

Brent was scared and angry. His face was bright red, and the words leapt out of his mouth at record speed. "We're going to have a serious talk, Adeline." I knew I was in big trouble when he addressed me as Adeline. "I called Dale," he continued, "but I had to leave a message."

The elevators opened, and six animal control officers jumped out. They looked like they were dressed for a trip to Mars. One of them—the leader, I suppose—asked, "What's the situation here?"

Brent spoke up, "As far as I know, Mr. Larceny is shut up in his office with two alligators."

"Three," I corrected. "Apparently, Lars thought he had two females, but he actually had a male and a female, who went on to have a baby. You won't believe all that went down tonight, but the bottom line is that Expert Doc came in drunk with a gun. It sounded like he wanted to shoot Lars, but his aim was off, and he shot the alligator tank instead. Doc got out, but Lars was drugged and unable to get out."

"Okay. That's all I need to know for now. I want the offices evacuated. Everyone down to the lobby except you two," the animal control officer said, addressing the medics. "You guys wait here. I imagine the gentleman in there is beyond help, since he's closed in there with three alligators, but stand by just in case."

We took the elevator down with four of the animal control officers, who returned carrying three extremely large cages. Brent began the drill, but I intervened.

"Listen, Brent, there's no reason we can't do this at my place. Mom is pretty shaken up. Let's get her home and warm. I've got my car. Can you follow me?"

***

At home, I took Mom up to my flat. Her cottage needed to be straightened up. Meanwhile,

I'd put her in my guest room. I went down to the cottage and got her pajamas and toiletries and made sure the place was secure. Back at my flat, I phoned Dale again, but had to leave a message with his service, so I paged him as well. I made hot toddies and put on some squash soup to warm. Mom took a hot shower and changed into her pajamas and robe. She came out looking like a pumpkin in her fluffy, soft, orange robe that she'd picked up in Ashland last summer. I love that robe, and Mom looks so adorable in it. Dale phoned back and as calmly as I could, I gave him the short version of what had taken place.

"Why didn't you call me before running over to Lars's office? That was a crazy thing to do," he chewed me out.

"I'm sorry, I was so worried about Mom, I just reacted," I replied.

"Addeline…" he hesitated. "I won't say any more. I'm on my way. I'll be there in ten minutes."

***

Brent received a call from the animal control guys saying that Lars didn't make it, but the alligators were contained and too fat and happy to put up much of a fight getting into their cages. Jaime and Chris had heard us come in and immediately wanted to know what was going on. Dale arrived and threw his arms around Mom and me, hugging us tightly and lecturing me on the dangers of running off on my own under such circumstances. I knew he was scared and angry and wanted to say more, but he also knew I was scared and upset, so he held his tongue. We all sat in front of the fireplace, holding our hot toddies, while Mom relayed her story and Brent took notes.

"I was prepping my mise en place for the Halloween cookies I'm making for the AAUW bake sale when Lars stormed into the kitchen. No, Addie, I didn't lock the door. Sorry. And I wasn't wearing that ugly necklace thing either. I grabbed the frying pan and tried hitting him on the head with it, but he's taller than I am, so I missed his head, but I hit his shoulder, which knocked the wind out of him.

"He grabbed his shoulder, and I ran around him into the living room to get out the front door. Lars was on my tail, so I threw pillows at him. He tripped on one and fell across the front door, blocking my escape. So, I hightailed it into my office, locking the door behind me. While Lars was banging on the door, I opened the window, pushed the screen out, and tumbled out onto the grass with the thought of running down the street, but Lars knocked the door down, jumped out the window, and grabbed me before I could even stand up."

I was breathless just listening. Mom continued, "Lars tied and gagged me, and tossed me in the back seat of his car. Did you know he has a 1939 Packard Roadster? I know because my dad had one of those back in the day. I used to model for their advertisements. It's one heck of a nice car, you know—soft leather seats, and I didn't feel a bump in the road riding to his offices. Maybe we should approach Mrs. L. about buying it.

"Anyway, we got to his parking garage. He parked the car, and I decided to pretend I'd passed out to make it harder for him to get me upstairs. I don't weigh much, but it's a lot of dead weight. Oops! Thank goodness I wasn't dead.

"Well, he just picked me up and threw me over his shoulder. I guess he decided that wouldn't look too good if someone saw us, so he got a blanket out of his trunk and wrapped me in that. That was awful. I had a hard time breathing. Anyway, then he threw me over his shoulder again and took me upstairs, where he unwrapped me and sat me down in a chair. I was flopping around and even fell on the floor because, remember, I was pretending to be passed out. I was hoping he'd leave me on the floor. It was better than being tied to the chair. But, he didn't. He got me in the chair and tied me to it. I scooched down as much as I could so that I wouldn't be tied too tightly to the chair. Then he reached over the desk, grabbed the phone, and called Addie.

"Addie arrived in what seemed like only a few minutes. I couldn't pretend to be passed out any longer because I knew that would scare her. What happened from there was a blurry whirlwind of activity. If I hadn't heard it all first-hand, I'd never believe it. Addie, you pick up the story. I want to drink my hot toddy before it cools off."

I relayed the story from there. The evening's events, like *A Comedy of Errors*, seemed like something you'd see on the stage at the Oregon Shakespeare Festival.

Chapter 32: Halloween
Thursday, October 31, 1996

I woke up early, though I'd rather have stayed in bed. I was sore from struggling with Lars and being dragged across the floor. My shoulder was much improved from the night's rest, but I put it back in the sling to keep it isolated. I started coffee and went into the guest room to check on Mom. She was gone. I threw on some sweats and ran down to the cottage where I found her baking cookies.

"What are you doing?" I exclaimed.

"For goodness' sake. What does it look like I'm doing? I have to get these cookies in the oven for the Halloween bake sale today."

"Right. That was a dumb question. What I meant was, I thought you'd be in bed today, nursing your injuries."

"Oh, no. My wrists are sore from the ropes, but other than that, I'm in good shape. This place is a mess, though, so I called Rosa, and she's coming over at ten o'clock to help clean up."

"Good thinking, Mom," I said, pouring myself a cup of coffee and grabbing a cookie.

"Uh-uh! Hands off the cookies. They're for the sale."

"I'm going to check with Jaime to see if he was able to get someone to cover my depos today and tomorrow. I want to rest my shoulder, and I should get an X-ray. I'll give Dale a call, too." I snuck another cookie and slunk out of the cottage. "Love you, Mom."

Before going upstairs to call my brother, I stopped at Jaime's. He said that Mary could cover my depo today, and she knew of a reporter who could cover the depo tomorrow. As I turned to walk out the door, Dale came into Jaime's office.

"How are you feeling this morning? Did you get your arm X-rayed? How is Mom? She wasn't in your flat. Where is she?" He was full of questions and concern.

"I feel fine. It's too early to have gotten my arm X-rayed. Mom is in her kitchen baking cookies. Good morning, Little Brother?"

We laughed and he gave me a hug. "I'm sorry," he said. "I've just been worried sick about you and Mom."

"I'm sorry, too," I said. "We were all upset. Brent will be on my case for months to come."

"I'll go see Mom, and you get that arm X-rayed. How does it feel this morning?" added Dale.

"My arm's fine. My shoulder's a tiny bit sore, but it'll be okay. I don't think anything's broken."

"I want you to run through what happened," Dale said. "I didn't get the full story last night."

Jaime interrupted us, "Come into the kitchen, you two. I've got coffee, and I'm going to rustle up some eggs. You can finish the conversation while you eat."

We drank dark, rich French roasted coffee and ate sumptuous omelets while I once again related the events of last night. The lawyer in my brother wanted to make sure he didn't miss any detail. I had to back-pedal a bit to get him up to speed.

"For Pete's sake," he said. "I leave town for a couple of weeks and all hell breaks loose around here."

"It has been quite a month," I said. "I promise to keep you in the loop from now on. The whole mess began while you were out of town, and it just sort of crept up on me. Anyway, what have you got going on today?"

"Great Scott! Look at the time. I've got to get to the office. I'm meeting with a client at eleven o'clock. I'll go over to Mom's on my way out."

"Okay. Don't steal any cookies or you're liable to get your hand slapped. Let's meet up later for the parade," I prompted.

"Yes. I wouldn't miss it for anything," Dale replied. "The parade begins at 5:30, so I'll have Viceroy pick us up at 4:30 so you and Mom can get settled in the float. Did I tell you that Burke retired, and I hired Viceroy for the limo driver position? He's a nice kid. I met him lifting weights. Everyone calls him Vice for short. He's got a great sense of humor."

"We met him briefly when he picked us up for the Halloween party. He's terrific," I said. Dale keeps a driver on his payroll so that he doesn't waste time sitting in traffic. He gets in an average of seven billable hours a week working on case files in the back seat of the limo.

206

I gave Dale a hug goodbye and cleaned up the kitchen for Jaime while he went back to his office. The Halloween activities started downtown just before noon so that the workers in the offices and stores could participate during their lunch hour. I went to check with Mom to see what time she wanted to drop off her cookies.

"11:30," she said. "I signed us both up for the 11:30 to 1:30 shift in the AAUW booth. Be sure to wear your Halloween shirt, and the black-and-orange scarf you knit with the adorable cap to match, and your Halloween sweater I knit for you a few years ago. You just look too precious for words in that darling outfit."

I'll look like a scarecrow, I thought, but said, "Okay, I'm on it, Mom. Give me forty-five minutes."

I went home, showered, and dressed as instructed, put on a bit of makeup and was back at the cottage in forty minutes. Mom was dressed almost as my twin. She loved the mother-and-daughter dresses and outfits of the '50s. We packed ten boxes of Halloween-decorated cookies in Mini and took off for downtown. I found the perfect parking spot. Since I took "est," Werner Erhard's self-improvement course, my parking karma has been at a high.

Working at the AAUW bakery booth was a ton of fun. We saw old friends and met new ones. Mom's cookies sold out quickly, but other volunteers brought pastries in every few minutes, so we had plenty to sell. It seemed like I snapped my fingers, and it was 1:30. "Let's go check out the other booths," I said to Mom.

"Yes, let's," she agreed. We strolled down the plaza, stopping at the various booths loaded with candy, crafts, knitwear, photography, paintings, books, and vintage items. I bought a Hopalong Cassidy lunch pail for Dale. He loved his, but it got grungy to the point of being unsanitary, so Mom had to throw it away. I knew he'd be thrilled to have this one. Mom found a complete set of embroidered Days of the Week dish towels. We've both had sets of those through the years, but they wore out. Mom saw one of her tennis buddies at the candy booth and went over to talk to her. As I wandered on, I caught sight of Kelly running toward me.

"Addie," he exclaimed, out of breath, "what the heck happened last night? I heard that you were abducted."

"Not abducted, really; I just rather walked into it. Lars called me and said he had Mom, and he wanted the envelope in return for her safety, so I hightailed it over to his office where he ambushed me and tied me up." I finished the story from there.

"Good grief, girl!" Kelly exclaimed. "That's a whole bunch of excitement. So, Lars and Expert Doc killed Hank Gould back in college so that Lars could marry Mrs. L. for her money. Then Lars killed Jonesy because he had evidence against him and couldn't be trusted, especially since he was leaving Lars's firm."

"Yep," I replied. "Then Expert Doc attempted a hit-and-run, hoping to kill Lars and set himself free from his hold. It isn't conclusive about who poisoned Expert Doc, but my theory is that he poisoned himself to throw suspicion on Lars."

"Do tell!" Kelly exclaimed. "That's crazy! He could have killed himself."

"Not really," I returned. "That particular poison is expelled from the body within twelve hours, and he also would have known that he'd get help right away, have his stomach pumped, and be home free. The police identified Expert Doc's Mercedes as the car that tried to hit me and did all the damage to the other cars. Expert Doc was probably afraid I was getting close to putting everything together. And he likely drained the brake fluid from Mini as well."

"Then who poisoned Keith? And why?" Kelly wondered aloud.

"That could have been anyone, but most likely Lars or Expert Doc. Dale's patio can be accessed from the beach, so anyone could have put on a costume and slipped in. It wouldn't have been difficult to put some poison into a drink. Whoever did it thought Keith was Appel and that Appel would most likely figure out their insurance fraud scheme before too long. It's just unthinkable, though, that Dale's young associate died due to mistaken identity."

"Geez! It makes me sick," he said.

"Me, too!"

We were interrupted by Hottie, Kelly's new love.

"Hey, Kelly," he said, "I've been looking all over for you. We need to get home and change for the parade."

"Oh, goodness, look at the time," I said. "I've got to find Mom and get home so we can get our costumes on as well. We're supposed to meet at our floats at five o'clock. See you guys later."

I found Mom at the booth selling Thanksgiving decorations and paper goods. She had a bundle she'd just finished paying for. "Hi, sweetie," she said. "I just bought a bunch of Thanksgiving stuff to take up to Kat's."

"That's so nice, Mom. Kat loves to decorate and make everything look festive. She takes after you. That bag looks heavy. Let me carry it for you. We should head home and get into our costumes."

"Right," Mom replied. "Dale is picking us up at 4:30. Let's go."

***

Promptly at 4:30, Mom and I met in the front of the house. Mom dressed as a tomato. She wore black leggings, and a balloon-like tomato covered her from her neckline to just below her knees. To top off the outfit, she wore a green fascinator displaying a stem and leaves. I was laughing, "Mom, that is so original."

"Well," she said. "Jaime gave me the idea when he talked about the gal throwing tomatoes last year. You look terrific, Addie. That's a '40s outfit, but I'm not placing who you are."

"Brenda Starr, Reporter, from the 1940s comic strip." I wore a red cotton sheath dress, '40s style, which fell below my knees. My accessories consisted of a belt at the waist and a red ribbon-type bow at the neckline. I wore a wig of long red hair, a red hat with a veil, white gloves, and red high heels. To complete the costume, I carried a pencil and notepad.

Vice pulled the limo into the driveway, and Dale jumped out wearing a black suit with a matching vest, a white shirt and bow tie, a dark brown hairpiece with a fake beard, and a top hat. Stumped, I couldn't figure out who he was until Mom yelled out, "Abraham Lincoln!"

"Oh, my goodness! It's perfect. Country lawyer. We must send a picture to Uncle Bud. Let me run up and get my camera," which I did, and we proceeded to take each other's pictures.

Vice dropped us off at the floats near the beginning of the parade. We rode in Dale's law firm's float, but he advertised Henkey Court Reporters as well. A couple of his junior partners, his paralegal, and his receptionist were already on board wearing various costumes. We laughed and waved to people gathered on the sidelines. As fog rolled in, I spotted a man with graying hair, dressed as the Lone Ranger, walking with a slight limp away from the floats and into the fog. I tried to focus, and then my heart skipped a beat. Gabe?

***

Following the parade, as is our custom, we all gathered at Dale's where Pete and Thelma had prepared appetizers, soup, salad, game hens stuffed with a spicy rice, sautéed squash, and pumpkin pie for dessert. As we were finishing our meal, and as if on cue, the phone rang. Pete answered, "Kat, how are you? We'd love to join the family for Thanksgiving, but we've promised Thelma's sister a visit...I will, and you have a great time." He handed the phone to me, "She's asking for you, Addie."

"Sweetie! How are you?" I said. "I'll put you on speaker, if that's okay, because everyone wants to hear what you have to say. We're at Uncle Dale's for our post-parade dinner. Thelma made her specialty, stuffed game hens."

"Hi, everyone," Kat replied. "I miss you all so much. I can hardly wait for Thanksgiving vacation. Granddad will be here, too."

"We're excited about coming up. Grandma and I plan to stay on for a week," I said. "Did you have many trick-or-treaters there in Lake Oswego?"

"Oh, yes, quite a lot. Puppy loved greeting all the kids, but now she's exhausted and sound asleep."

"Sweetie, let me call you tomorrow. I have some logistics concerning Thanksgiving weekend that I want to discuss with you."

"Sounds good, Mom. Love you."

"Love you, too, Kats!"

***

Soon we were saying goodnight as we climbed into the limo. Dale and Pete and Thelma walked out with us. Pete gave me a hug and said, "Now, listen, promise me you'll keep out of trouble while you're up at Kat's."

"Really, Pete, what could possibly happen in sleepy little Lake Oswego?"

Epilogue

Baxter and his mom won the lawsuit against Lars's law firm. They purchased a villa in Palermo, Sicily, with their three-million-dollar settlement. Baxter met a lovely lady who made his mom a grandma. Grandma B. opened a knitting shop, exporting hand-knit baby garments.

Expert Doc escaped the country, landing in the small retirement village of Ajijic, Jalisco, Mexico, where he leads AA groups for alcoholic retirees.

Norma had a baby girl and named her Adeline. She and Mrs. L. are living happily ever after in their quaint little five-thousand-square-foot Beverly Hills home. As it turns out, Mrs. L. wasn't as dumb as Lars made her out to be; she'd been redirecting money from Lars's law firm into her own account for years. As for Norma leaving her previous employment under suspicious circumstances, I never did learn what that was all about, perhaps just idle gossip.

And, poor Lars. Mrs. L. had an elaborate funeral ceremony for him. What was left of him was buried under a lovely *Conium maculatum* plant—otherwise known as poison hemlock—at Mount Sinai Memorial Park. Following the funeral, Mrs. L. threw a party for two thousand people at the Beverly Hills Hotel and had it catered by Wolfgang Puck. She wore an Oscar de la Renta floral lace-appliqué wedding dress, and, though not a legal marriage by current law, she and Norma were married at Lars's funeral reception.

Me? I wrote a play based on the case and the events of the evening Mom and I were kidnapped. The reviews say, "Adeline Henkey has written a comedy to beat all. Move over, Neil Simon." It was produced at the Oregon Shakespeare Festival. My date for opening night was Jon, the gentleman who rescued me the night my brakes failed on Mini. Oh, yes! The court reporter always does get the last word.

The End

Made in the USA
Middletown, DE
26 August 2024